Nykkynn's

CATACLYSMA

{Pre-Editor Edition}

Fantasy Adventure Comedy

Cover Art by Daniel Jacobs Nykkynn

ISBN 978-0-578-73063-9
Published and printed by
Amazon on Demand

DEDICATION

I dedicate this book to the human race,
myow're not perfect but myow make great
servants.

ESSENCES

Immersive Audiobook

Audiobook Time Total: 185m: 23s
Potential Reading Time: **3 hrs: 5m: 23s**

1 ● RACOONIANS

It was the middle of the night and the only thing a lit was the moon reflecting on the ocean horizon, as a couple of speeder boats roar through the water and around the back side of an island in the Tropics. They meet at a discrete dockside in the darkness along the cliff-face-beach, dimly lit by the lights of a few other speeder boats roped to the wood. The Speeder docks, and the American Shorthair Cats **standing on all 4s** onboard, step onto the surface dressed in Fishing outfits yet, having the physique of soldiers; they were dirty and mangy, yet muscular. They meet with cats wearing black suits with black beanies, Lucky *the Ragdoll cat*, Charlie *the Scottishfold cat* and Whiskers *the Persian White cat*. They shake paws together and start loading boxes of Nip from the boat to the dock and one of the Cats picks up his radio and calls it in, "Mr. Cataclysma, the cargo has been received." The ominously deep dark voice on the other side of the radio says, "Good." and laughs cynically, "Ehehehe!" The Speeder boats all dispatch from the dock and ride off into the night on the ocean.

Elsewhere among the island, a Space Police Saucer hovers silently among the hill with red and blue lights flashing at the top, where the team of Cats inside are being debriefed. They wore Astronaut suits with Cop Badges. Their bubble helmets were off and they're being debriefed by Ms. Twinkle Toes; she is the lead of the Space Police Team. She wears a suit as well and standing before the podium with the screen buzzing pictures behind her, she speaks to them, "Alright, for the millionth time, listen up everyone. Since the great Cat Monument Collapse, we've gone high tech so the Nip runners have gone low. Sources say the biggest shipment of Nip is comin' in tonight and we wanna know who's behind it and in a few hours… we will."

The screen behind her changes to a layout map of the striking point their going after, and she turns to face it, presenting with her paw out, "We're going to come at them from 3 points. Water team, Vehicle team, and On foot. We cannot make any mistakes on this mission, so we cannot make a move until the Head Officers identify the Nip, and call it in. These guys we're after, they've got a lot of fire power and they hate the law… so keep myow eyes dilated out there."

The Speeder zooms through the water as Space Police Cats mobilize throughout the island, beaming down in complex arrangement among the trees of the darkness and the sounds of the birds. A swarm of 10 Cats in Astronaut outfits with cop badges holding machine guns aimed ahead, mobilizing into position. "Bravo is in position, over." One of the Space Cop Cats say. A unit off the west holds position in the bushes with one of them wearing infrared binoculars, speaking into the radio, "Boat incoming." As the Speeder boat roars through the water towards the point of expectation. There is a beach side with a bonfire and a bunch of different racoons dressed in all robes that look like white shiny plastic trash bags, standing around the fire. There was possibly 30 of them there. The leader of the group wears something made of Potato Chip Bags; he raises his paws into the air before the fire and says, "Brothers! Gather with me now!"

The Boat roars to the beach and ports with the dock there where one of the racoon group members meets Whiskers the Persian White on the boat. Whiskers complains,

"Why didn't myow tell me there was going to be this shit here tonight?"

The racoon member throws his paw into the air and says, "Racoonian power!"

Whiskers looks confused and tosses a box of Nip to the member, and speeds off in the boat while their ceremony began. Suddenly, two of the members throw off their Trash Bag suits and reveal themselves to be Space Cops! Oscar *the thin Orange Tabby Cat*, and Muffins *the Gradient Grey Maine Coon Cat*! In their Dark Blue Space Cop Casual wear, they both point their guns at the members quickly and yell in his 'Surf's Up' Keanu accent, "Space Police! No body move!"

"It's a couple of Pussies!" one of the Racoon yells in shock!

"Call me a Pussy again, Mother Myowker." Muffins says calmly in his meat-headed Arnold Austrian accent, pointing the guns right at the Racoon's head. "Drop the box," Muffins says sternly at the member holding the box of Nip. The Racoon immediately drops it.

Oscar calls it in, "Alpha leader, bring the pounce!"

"Repeat myow transmission." Alpha leader responds. Static. "Alpha team to

Brovo unit, please continue relay."

Oscar yells into the radio! "Alpha-Bring in that pounce!" It's all static.

The Racoons smile deviously and Muffins says, "It's all static. The radios are myowked."

One of the racoons starts laughing and Oscar brings the gun closer to the racoon's face, "What's so funny, meow?"

"Oscar!" Muffins yells, "Where are they?"

One of the racoons makes a run for it! Oscar trips him and the racoon falls flat on his face! Suddenly another racoon pulls out a gun and grabs distracted Oscar and holds him hostage at gun point with Muffins watching it switch up, Muffins starts groaning and pointing his gun everywhere in a panic, ready to shoot anyone as they all back off and the Racoon with the hostage smiles insidiously! "Okay, myow want to make this more interesting?" Oscar asks "Let's make it more interesting!"

"Put my colleague down," Muffins says in his big commando voice, "or I'll pop myow head like a bubble."

"You ain't gonna shoot, Pussy!" the racoon yells.

Muffins interjects, "Just because

myow got my partner right now, doesn't mean I won't pop myow face."

"It's all talk." The racoon says.

"What myow don't know," Muffins says looking around and back at the main racoon swiftly and alert, "is that my partner came here ready to lose one of his 9 lives."

Oscar looks confused, "Dude, I got shit to do tomorrow."

Muffins insists, "I'm going to blow a hole through my partner to open up myow silly racoon face and push all myow bullshit aside so I can see the view past myow stupid neck."

"Dude!" Oscar freaks out, "I got a bitch waitin' for me!"

"I'll make myow a deal," Muffins says, "Myow tell me who gave myow the box of Nip and maybe I'll just slash myow face a few times instead! Or myow can keep acting like a myowkin' racoon and I can blow myow head off!"

"OR," Oscar cuts him off, "we sit down and deescalate the situation by talking about it like grown adults with highly developed maturity and spiritual understanding!"

"Myow'll have to forgive my partner," Muffins clarifies, "He's been demasculated recently and it's affecting his ability to represent us properly."

Off in the bushes the Space Cop Cat Units are trying to make out what's happening, "I think there's some shit going down!"

"Hold myow positions!" Alpha leader insists.

"The racoon has a gun to my head!" Oscar yells at Muffins.

"He'll put it down when I put a bullet in his snout!" Muffins yells.

The Racoon squirms, "Keep talkin', ya cocky pussy! See if it get's ya anywhere!"

"Just calm down, Muffins!" Oscar pleas.

"I am calm, look at me, I'm calm–" suddenly one of the other racoons moves and Muffins quickly starts pointing his guns everywhere, "–Something moved! Something moved! I am way too stressed out for this shit right now! Do myow understand me?? Everybody stop moving or I'll start poppin' everyone's bubbles!"

"Look! Dude! Dude!" Oscar tries to stop all the madness, "We can just all go back to the Protective Space Police Station

Patrol Ship and work it out fairly in a court of law. Doesn't that sound reasonable?"

"We've got lawyers!" the racoon yells. "They've never once finished a court case!"

"What the myowk are myow talking about?" Muffins asks irritable.

"Don't look at me- it's Muffins!" Oscar pleas, "He's crazy! Look at him! I don't know what he's gonna do next!"

"Put the gun down." Muffins says.

Oscar continues headlocked as a hostage still with the gun pressed up to his fuzzy head, "This mother myowker has emotions he's not in touch with, dude! He found out his Dad is part Liger! It's myowkin' traumatic!"

"1." Muffins says with the gun pointed at the racoons head.

Oscar pleas again, "This guy's aim is like, really good but like, not that good! So if like he misses, like, he'll still myowk myow up!"

"2!"

"Muff – NO!"

"Hail Racoonia!"

The racoon behind them grabs a shotgun and cocks it quickly and Muffins spins around and fires blowing a massive hole in the racoons chest. Blood splashes everywhere painting Muffins red! He turns back around quickly and fires the gun again as everyone scrambles – the bullet hits the hostage-ing racoon in the head and it explodes like 'Scanners'! The rest of the Police team is immediately alerted by the gun fire and move in quickly! It turns into a huge shootout between cats and racoons!

Oscar breaks free- jumping behind some boxes and firing his gun at some of the racoons blasting at his way! Sparks flare by his shoulder and he ducks down quickly as more shots are fired from his right! Outside the beachside, the Ambush moves in on boat and Saucer while the ground team starts firing its way into the shootout! Oscar is firing rapidly at his assailants as he spazzes to another location to take cover, and pops off shots at the racoons behind him, hitting a gas tank as it explodes into a ball of flames!

Muffins is grabbing racoon after racoon, putting them in a head lock, and then snapping their necks, one by one, as if in line for a neck snapping. Oscar yells, "Muffins!" as a racoon jumps out with a shotgun ready to fire at Muffins, and Oscar jumps to a better angle firing quickly, blowing the racoon's head clean off with blood spraying everywhere like a broken lawn sprinkler!

Muffins looks up and realizes Oscar saved him as another racoon steps up behind Oscar with a gun ready to fire and Muffins yells "Oscar!" firing his gun rapidly, putting train tracks across the racoons belly as he falls over and splashes into a pool of his own blood!

The Space Police team surges the beach and the racoons immediately surrender with their paws in the air – the Cats put them to the ground with their paws behind their back as they paw cuff them. Lights flash everywhere with such a raid, as Oscar and Muffins stand in the middle breathing heavy, exhausted, roughed up, dirty, but accomplished.

"They may take our lives," Oscar says, "but they'll never take the other 8."

2 ● SPECIAL PUSSIES

When the Space Police Saucer returns from the Cat Planet into Space, they come upon their mothership, the Protective Space Police Station Patrol Ship or the 'PSPSPS' pronounced "Psss-psss-psss" for short. The Ship resembled a glass box, and from the center to the corner of the glass box was more boxes with other boxes inside the boxes inside those boxes, connected by tubes as if thousands of satellites connected by glass hamster tubes.

The Space Police Saucer goes into a garage door on the side corner of the PSPSPS, that then goes into the box itself and encloses the ship into a sort of "room" of the box, large enough for the ships to use as a kind of parking lot, parking ships right at the dockside of satellite boxes. At the garage door, inside the containment before being released into the glass box, the gas in the chamber is exchanged into oxygen, and then the other door opens to let the saucer into the PSPSPS glass box structure. Inside, the saucer lands on the 'Tilapia' landing pad and the crew *and captured criminals,* all migrate into the space station.

Oscar and Muffins walk into the office of Ms. Twinkle Toes *a white Himalayan cat*, and they sit down facing Ms. Twinkle Toes who looks so cute and sweet, tends to speak quite the contrary. "So, can I ask myow a question?" she asks them.

"Yes." Muffins says.

"Why the hell did we send an entire team of Police squad to seize a box of Catnip and a gang of Racoonians?"

Oscar puts his paw up like he knows the answer, "Bargaining power!"

"No!" she yells, "There was no good reason! But myow're in luck, because if it wasn't for me, myow entire raid would've been a waste of time."

"Get to the myowking point, Ms. Twinkle Toes." Muffins was tired.

"The symbols and types used on the box are linked to Maximus Cataclysma." Ms. Twinkle Toes explain, "The most notorious Murderer and Evil Mastermind villain in the entire Galaxy."

"So like, are myow saying he's on cat planet then?" asked Oscar.

"We don't know where he is, but

we've definitely found a trace to him connecting to the 'SS Pussy Willow'. All we needed to locate more Catnip with these symbols and find out who's bringing them to this planet, was this raid. And myow can thank me later too, because if it wasn't for this link, I would've fired both of myow."

"Yeah well myowk myow too, lady." Muffins says.

"Well, that's why I like working here," Oscar says, "because this place provides a real sense of job security."

"I don't think the two of myow will be enough against Cataclysma," Twinkle Toes says, "but I definitely don't need to expend an entire crew of Police to take care of something like this either, so I'm going to build myow team. But myow'll need to watch myow backs in the meantime. Anyone who is a threat to Cataclysma will be under constant attack by his henchcats until myow're completely eliminated."

"Don't worry." Muffins says, "I'm gonna pound that cake like it's my birthday."

"I've already recruited the first of this special team." Ms. Twinkle Toes says, "her name is Shallow." She shows the file of her to them with the photograph *of a British*

Blue cat.

Oscar does a victory punch to the sky, "Aw yeah! Got some new butt to play with!"

Ms. Twinkle Toes didn't stop there, she travelled to Meow York on the Cat planet seeking a Special Agent. Inside the building of Secret Sassy Services, and after meeting with several of the board members, she stands outside the Capitol of Meow York and awaits *the Bicolor Manx Tuxedo cat*... Oreo 7. He arrives wearing a tuxedo and tie, looking formal and handsome. Ms. Twinkle Toes meets with him and they walk together along the sidewalk out front, "Myow are Ms. Twinkle Toes I presume." Oreo 7 says.

"Yes," she says, "But I don't think I caught myow name."

"Kitty kitty." He says, "Here Kitty kitty. But myow can call me Oreo 7."

"Is that Detroit-ish?" she asked.

He hesitated... "Yes."

She goes on, "Myow assignment is to work with a team of professional Space Police officers to hunt down and arrest

Maximus Cataclysma. Myow transportation will be provided and what have myow."

"Who is Maxmimus Cataclysma?" Oreo 7 asks.

"He's the Criminal and homicidal maniacal murderer and mastermind behind the cult suicides, bombings, and unwanted rapes leading to murder. The cat is an absolute menace. Having found a connection like this could mean the bringing down of the Galaxy's most dangerous villain."

Oreo 7 grinds his teeth, "Oh geez, that gives me a real rocket ship; I'm in."

3 ● STALKER CHARLIE

In the PSPSPS, in the hustle and bustle of cyberpunk kitties getting to work with their ultra-technology cruising around all the box units connected to each other inside the glass box Mothership, Oscar and Muffins walk among the crowd. Muffins suddenly notices they're being followed. Oscar and Muffins stop at the corner of the walk and Muffins says, "Don't look, but there's somebody following us and I said don't look so don't look around just look straight ahead and forward and DO NOT look behind us." Oscar looks back and around to examine the area. "Myow suck."

"What do we do?" Oscar asks.

"Follow me, I know what to do." Muffins says.

Its Charlie, one of the cats that dropped off a box of Nip back at the crime scene that night. Well here he is now, spying. Muffins takes Oscar all the way to the Vatoport, and up to the teller where he gets Oscar and himself a ticket to ride the Televator out to the edge of the PSPSPS called 'Teown'. They receive their tickets as

Charlie watches from far away and they walk into the station, boarding the Televator car which was set to leave in 5 more minutes. Charlie runs up to the ticket booth and buys himself a ticket, boarding as well, and taking his seat towards the back of the Televator car, spying upon Oscar and Muffins up at the front. With the magnificent Space Station Scape out the window, Muffins panics in a low profile.

"There he is." Muffins says.

"Now what?" Oscar asks.

"Go to the bathroom." Muffins says.

"Right here? Right now?"

"No, myow idiot," Muffins says to him sternly, "When I say go, that means get up off myow butt and take it to another location. Stop myowking around and go to the bathroom."

Oscar got up and walked back down the isle towards the back of the car where a bathroom is similarly to that of a human airline jet. Muffins gets up, and calmly strolls over to Charlie who is sitting down and getting himself adjusted still, not noticing Muffins yet. Muffins sits down next to Charlie, and still Charlie is too distracted to notice Muffins, preoccupied by the window, the seat, the table, the recline, the space, the whole thing was a little uncomfortable, and Muffins suddenly swat Charlie in the face repeatedly, SWAT! SWAT! SWAT! SWAT! SWAT! SWAT! SWAT SWAT SWAT SWAT! Charlie is unconscious, laying there with his tongue hanging out and the stewardess walks up, "Is everything okay here?"

Muffins smiles calmly, "Yea, I'm doin' great. How long is the ride?"

"From here to Teown is about 2 minutes."

"Great." Muffins says, "Listen, my friend here had a long day. Try not to disturb him…"

"Not a problem sir, he'll be just fine." the Stewardess says.

"Thank myow," Muffins says and the Stewardess walks back up the isle of the Televator.

Muffins gets up and walks towards the back of the train and knocks on one of the bathroom stalls. Oscar walks out of another and says, "What happened?"

"He gave it a rest." Muffins says.

They both exit the Televator train quickly, and the doors shut behind them. They watched it take off, but another cat by the name of Lucky was close by watching

from around the corner and smiles and says,
"clever cat."

4 ● PSYCHO GENIUS

Walking through a corridor of the Furbaltimore Asylum, Dr. Tiger *a Toyger cat*, and Shallow a *British blue cat*, descend into the bowels of the hospital, with iron gates clanking shut behind them. Dr. Tiger is a cat dressed much as a professor might dress with brown suit and red bow tie, however Shallow is a Space Police Investigator and she wears the dark blue uniform respectfully. "Many cats have come to meet the Doctor." Tiger says, "But not many are successful at forming a bond of trust or getting any cooperation."

"I'm unorthodox." Shallow says, "At least that's what I hope to bring to the table."

"And myow're here on behalf of…?" he awaited…

"The Space Police are developing a Special team to seek out and hunt down a criminal that Dr. Bonkers may have some information on." Shallow says.

"Why did Ms. Twinkle Toes send *myow* to me though?" Dr. Tiger asks, "If he knows that Dr. Bonkers won't talk to myow?"

"Myow don't know that." She says.

"Cats are suckers for hope." Dr. Tiger says. While walking, Dr. Tiger describes, "Dr. Bonkers is a peculiar patient that is described as being cold and… much like a snake. He's a lot like Jekyll and Hyde, he may seem like myow friend now, but the moment he's free to do as he pleases, he shows his true self. He's a consistent personality, not dual or multiple. Therefore, when he breaks, he goes into a rampage and destroys everything like a psychotic."

"I understand, Doctor." She says.

"*Do* myow?" he asks.

"I realize the severity of this meeting, Dr. Tiger." Shallow says, "I don't need the lecture."

"Yes myow do," Dr. Tiger insists, "There's logistics and rules for dealing with him. It's not a book, it's a serial killer, Ms. Shallow." He pulls out a gruesome picture of a victim to Dr. Bonkers and Shallow hisses at it. Dr. Tiger puts the picture back in his pocket, "Dr. Bonkers is not a cat, Ms. Shallow, he's… something else."

As they arrive at the ward which houses Bonkers, Shallow requests, "I'd like to go in alone. I may have more luck as an individual and wouldn't want other associations to dilute my efforts."

Her comment annoys him, but he acquiesces to her suggestion. He tells her that, "Bonkers is in the last cell. We've set out a chair for myow if myow need it." Pointing to a video monitor, Dr. Tiger reassures her that, "Security is watching and myow'll do fine."

Shallow sets down the long corridor, through the darkness with the cells containing mentally ill occupants on her left. She is accosted by Toby in one of the first cells, *a Lykoi cat* who says to her, "I can smell myow butt."

As she comes to Bonker's cell, she sees a near-empty enclosure with a few pieces of bolted-down furniture, and plenty of softcover books and walls adorned with detailed drawings — mostly scribbles. And, of course, the cell's lone occupant Dr. Bonkers, *a Selkirk Rex Cat*. The doctor sits up straight on his bunk in rainbow cloud and blue skies pajamas, pale and poised. He cordially greets Shallow wide eyed, "Hello."

"Good morning Dr. Bonkers, I'd like to speak with myow."

"Myow must be an underling of Ms. Twinkle Toes."

"That's correct," She says, "I'm

Detective Shallow with the Space Police."

"May I see myow credentials?" She flashes her flip up badge wallet and he glances noticing, "the temporary ID does not fool me, Ms. Shallow. It expires soon. Myow're not a Detective with the Space Police are myow?"

"I'm a Student at the Space Police Academy, interning for Space Police Investigations. My official badge is coming in soon."

"Twinkle Toes sent me a pupil?" Dr. Bonkers asks, "Pfft…"

"I'm here to learn Dr. Bonkers." She says clueless to the intimidation.

"Learn what?"

"Learn about what myow know." He looks on at her, impressed by her confidence in his presence, not realizing she's a complete airhead. "Myow used to work for Maximus Cataclysma." She says.

He's silent a moment and then says, "Have a seat."

She sits, and looks on at the pictures in the cell… they're a bunch of scribbles with crayons. She asks, "Are these myow drawings, Dr. Bonkers?"

"Yes."

"They're um… nice." She says.

"They're scribbles." He says.

She nods awkwardly… "I can see that. A lot of detail, all that just by memory?"

"It's all I can remember anymore." Dr. Bonkers says, "A bunch of scribbles."

"Well," she says with a chuckle, "Maybe myow can scribble on this Survey."

"Awe c'mon!" he yells going bat shit crazy in the cell and starts throwing shit everywhere… and then calms down, "I was just beginning to like myow Ms. Shallow. Myow were nice to me, received my thoughts respectfully… then myow pulled out a commercial. It's like myow don't even care what I'm watching, as long as I'm watching the myowking commercial. Myow were just working myow way up to it weren't myow? Myow spent like… 5 hours writing a shpeel on how to present it to me. Am I really talking to myow, or am I talking to a puppeteer?"

Shallow rolls her eyes, "I'm just asking myow to look at this survey, *geez*."

He looks on skeptically and sarcastically says, "Right, Twinkle Toes must be so busy if she's sending one of her students down here to ask me questions. Do myow know why they call him Maximus

Cataclysma? Do myow know why?"

"Because he wants to *create* a maximum cataclysm." She says.

"Why do myow think he removes their furcoat?" he asks.

"Because he's a Sphinx and he doesn't have fur of his own." She says.

He looks on casually and intrigued, "Gimme."

She put the stapled pages through the slot in the glass and he takes the paper, looking it over as she sits a moment and he says, "Detective Shallow, this survey is a piece of shit. Myowk myow survey. I'd rather shit on myow survey... Detective Shallow. And myow know what? I think I'm gonna switch it into high gear and go with a 'Myowk myow' too. Myow come in here with myow ideas and myow hope and myow dreams like I couldn't just set them on fire right now. Well they're burning, bitch. Myowk myow dreams. Myow wanna know what I hope. I hope myow succeed. Yeah. I do. I gotta plethora of hope. I mean, I don't myowkin' use it, maybe myow can. One cat's trash, is also trash for another cat."

She looks on at him uncomprehensive of everything he just said as if it was too much for her to pay attention to. She says with a nod, "That's nice." He looks confused, and she says, "So myow think myow are a God?"

"Test me bitch. Test me." He says. There's a pause. "I'll eat anything bitch. I ate Smokey. Remember Smokey? I ate him. I ate that mother myowker with rice and milk."

"Well I'm kind of crazy too!" she says enthusiastically…

"Bullshit."

"No, I'm serious. Sometimes there's so much pretty in the world, it makes me wanna scratch someone's face off." She says.

He ponders a moment, "Hmm… an intriguing confession… from myow who are… here for what reason?"

"We need myow to help the Space Police." She says. He's caught off guard. There's another pause.

"No."

She continues, "All myow've seen are these walls, myow can't even draw a picture without it being scribbles. I can get myow out of here, but on the condition that myow help the Space Police."

"For freedom, be a hypocrite." He says.

She shows him a picture of the SS Pussy Willow and says, "Myow could be here, helping us stop the very cat that put myow in this cell. Because if it wasn't for the fact that Max back stabbed myow to get away, myow'd still be free… eating other cats."

He screams, "Myow're a Liar!" It's quiet a moment. Shallows eyes are big and shocked, and he feels a sense of embarrassment... "There's no proof he backstabbed me."

She's quiet still, and then pulls out a picture and shows it to him as he looks on with his expression going from calm… to confusion… to depression… to absolute rage, "No! No! NO NO NO!!! NO!!" he bangs on the glass!

"Then will myow help us?" she asks again. He stops… and stares at her with crazed eyes…

5 ● TACO SPACE CITY

Oscar, Muffins, Shallow, Ms. Twinkle Toes, and Dr. Bonkers are in a conference room, with a window looking out into the glass Box of the PSPSPS and the vastness of space beyond. Dr. Bonkers is strapped on to a self-controlled mobile dolly in a straitjacket with a mouth guard; he can't move anything but control where he goes by the push of a few buttons under his paw, and he talks. That's it. Oscar and Shallow greet shaking paws, Muffins goes to shake paws with Dr. Bonkers but then walks away. There's a spark between Shallow and Oscar already, "Myow."

Oscar says to her, "Myow're so beautiful, it's painful."

"It's just myow eyes." She says.

"No" Oscar says, "I think it's my lungs. Who are myow?"

"I'm Shallow. I'm not a Princess but I like to be treated like one, I have daddy issues, and I might break my own morals for attention, I don't even know if I belong in this position, but if I do well, will myow take me for who I am?" She asks.

"Pfft- myowkin' A baby." Oscar says, "but only if myow don't have a bad attitude all the time, save that shit for the field. Myow an apprentice still learning the trade; myow gotta *earn* princess titles here." He presents a seat next to him with his paw out, "Please, have a seat."

Ms. Twinkle Toes stands in the room overlooking paperwork on the case. Oscar sits at the table and says, "No matter what we do, Cataclysma is going to drag it out. So how do we stop him?"

Muffins says, "He has an army of cats working behind him; henchcats."

Dr. Bonkers chuckles, "He's more equipped to handle this space station than myow may realize. He may as well have his own Sovereignty. That's why he uses Mr. Bigglesworth to do all of the labor."

Oscar asks, "Who is Mr. Bigglesworth?"

Shallow says, "He's the Original Gangster of the Puss City in the SS Pussy Willow. He's a Boss."

"Why does he use Mr. Bigglesworth?" Oscar asks.

Dr. Bonkers interjects, "Maybe it would be a lot easier to understand what's going on if we all just paid Mr. Bigglesworth a visit."

Shallow *a British blue*, Dr. Bonkers *a Selkirk Rex*, Oscar *the Orange Tabby* and Muffins *the Grey Maine Coon* take a saucer to SS Pussy Willow, not knowing what to expect. When they look out at the view of the massive mother ship orbiting the massive blue gas planet, it is absolutely, spectacular. The entire Mothership is one massive Taco, with massive windows where the meat, cheese and lettuce goes.

And inside the structure is a huge city on both sides, with massive lawns, fountains, monuments, buildings, monorails, societies of cats of all different domestic house cat cultures. They were all inside one massive taco space mothership. The windows even had a rainbow like gradient scale of brown, to yellow, to green, to clear, and then back; green yellow brown, from left to right, giving the illusion that the SS Pussy Willow Mothership… is a loaded Taco.

The Saucer approaches and they get a great view of the massive City Ship with the sun bouncing off its reflective yellowish

off white Taco Shell side, with the massive
blue gas giant behind it. The Saucer enters
the same way, in containment first, and then
let into the shell, where the City is formed
for yards and yards above and below, with
sky scrapers stretched from bottom to top,
whichever side that is to the perspective
from stand-point, but they otherwise called
one "A Side" and the other "B Side". And
the colors of the rainbow were lights along
the trims of walkways, building windows,
etc…

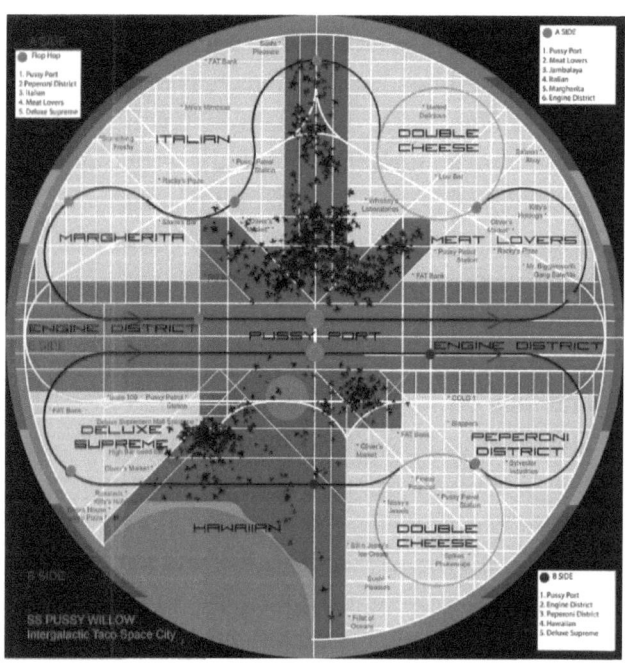

"This place is so beautiful!" Shallow says with amazement.

"Yes." Muffins says, "Unfortunately were headed towards the back of the ship... the bottom of the taco where the Engine District is... and the windows are brown."

They landed at the bottom of the Taco, where the windows were brown, on top of a landing pad, on top of a building that was facing in sideways, looking up towards the windows of the taco in the SS Pussy Willow. When they step off the Saucer from the steps out the door, the first thing they notice; "Oh my Hands!" Oscar yells, "What is that smell?"

"It's cat shit." Dr. Bonkers says bluntly, "Myow dummy. It's obviously the aroma of shit, how can it be questioned? This is where all the cat shit goes in the SS Pussy Willow."

"Where does it go from there?" Shallow asks.

Muffins says, "It gets flushed out into space during certain rotations, so that it falls towards the Gas Planet."

Bonkers immediately points out- "Because the Blue Planet is a massive toilet bowl to cat civilization."

"This is where Mr. Bigglesworth is?"

Shallow asks.

"No," Bonkers insists, "He's not here yet."

"What?" Oscar couldn't believe it, "We came out here to catch him!"

"And myow will, as soon as he arrives. We wait here out of sight until he gets here and then when he does, we'll head into the city where he is and catch him!"

6 ● CAT CHASE

"It licks itself clean like a good cat, it does this whenever it's told." Mr. Bigglesworth says, *a Calico cat*, and thug in Gangster apparel, cold crazy calm eyes, a cigar, bandana, and black backwards hat. He was looking down at a caged cat victim of his, 'Princess', a Savannah cat stripped down to her fur. It was an Elevator containment with room to move but Princess looked terrified.

"My family will pay myow whatever myow want to let me go!" she yells.

"It licks itself clean like a good cat, or else it gets the spray again." Mr. Bigglesworth says again sternly, holding his white pet mouse in his arms, and the hairspray water bottle in the other.

"Okay! Okay!" she says, and she begins to lick her arm… over and over…

Mr. Bigglesworth turns around and walks away from the elevator shaft that the caged hostage is being kept in, and exits into a control bridge looking out into space. The cat crew among Mr. Bigglesworth's Pirate Ship are all calico cats, but Mr.

Bigglesworth was obviously the Alpha. Among the Calico cat crew whom weren't calico cats because they were specifically picked for tasks, were 3 different cats. 'Shadow' was the black cat with yellow slit eyes dressed in all leather black, sitting to the right of Mr. Bigglesworth on deck. To the left of him, 'Cobalt', *the Russian blue cat*, dressed in all leather black wearing sunglasses. And, standing just beside and behind him, Cataclysma's representative, 'Pudder' the Siamese Cat dressed in a trench coat and fedora. They're all aboard a black and red trim spaceship that resembles a sleek yacht with a Pirate appearance that is entirely enclosed and has no sail. It's beat up, seen battles, has crossbones and cat skull stencil painted on the side.

The ship's size in comparison to the SS Pussy Willow is only a 40th of it's size, but as it comes to the gates, the ship is to large to enter, so Pirate hotdog shuttles are sent out from the Pirate ship. They were 3 hotdog shuttles full of Pirate Cats ready to raid the cat city inside; each hotdog shuttle leader 1 of the 3 specialty cats.

The ships cruise through No-Fly zones, all Pussy Patrol units are radioed immediately, "Space Pirates have entered the city! Code Raow! Code Raow!"

Oscar and Muffins hear it on their radios, "That's him!"

"Didn't take long, did it?" Dr. Bonkers says.

The Hotdog Shuttles fly through and shoot guns at random with screaming cats everywhere running frantically; like watching herds of the African Serengeti from a bird's-eye-view, moving in chaos theory across the hot planes above and below! The Shuttles touch down on 'B Side' in the Hawaiian District close to the roads of the Deluxe Supreme District and all the Calico cats get out wearing all black pointing their guns around the perimeter as Cobalt *the Russian Blue* exits the ship quickly and says, "Today's forecast... this spray." The Calico team follows behind him to assist! Shadow *the black cat*, and Pudder *the Siamese* follows.

They bash the doors into 'Oliver's Market *a Meat market,* and **an Exotic Shorthair cat** working behind the counter in his Asian accent, yells at the cats as they bust in, "o-uh-shit!" He runs away quickly! The Calicos begin looting the market of all it's meat by packing sacks full of chopped beef, pork, chicken, and fish!

Suddenly, Muffins and Oscar arrive on the scene and point their guns at the calico robbers inside! "Everybody freeze!" Muffins yells! The Calico cats all turn around and notice the two of them. They begin to slowly engage them as other Calicos got back to filling their bags. One of the Calicos grabs Muffin's paw and says, "Myow ain't nothin'!" attempting to pull him away, but Muffin twists his wrist around the Calico's grab and SWAT's him in the face! He turns to the other Calico and SWATs him in the face too! The other Calico pulls his gun up to shoot but Muffin jumps at the Calico, biting his head, and clawing up the Calico's chest with his back feet claws! The Calico leaps to safety quickly, running away!

Muffins sees Cobalt and Pudder on the run in the back, as the cats Exit the back door quickly! Muffins runs through the crowd of calico cats as shots are fired and he leads to the back with Oscar following behind him- the walls popping in gun shots and the market hitting a climax of chaos! They fly out the back door rapidly, running after Cobalt! Cobalt Looks behind him and sees them running after him, so he frantically pulls his gun out and begins firing back at them, forcing them to stop and take cover while he runs off! The Calicos start chasing behind the Space cops firing their guns off at Muffins and Oscar who immediately have to take cover on the other side of the building corner! Oscar fires back from the corner and one of the cats explodes like a watermelon full of C4! Oscar and Muffins hide behind the corner and as soon as the Calicos come around the corner, Muffins SWATs the shit out of all of them over and over, SWAT! SWAT SWAT! SWAT! SWAT! SWAT SWAT! SWAT SWAT! As they scatter into random directions and take off. Muffins and Oscar continue to chase after Cobalt and Pudder as he exits the alley ways out to the open street!

A crew of Pussy Patrol units in Turquoise uniforms start flooding the area as the Calicos begin to fight them, and a massive brawl breaks out in the alley! Muffins and Oscar run after Cobalt and Pudder as they exchange gun fire back and forth across the massive grass lawn park in Hawaiian!

Cobalt and Pudder runs up on an area full of cats wandering about to their daily lives coming up escalators as Cobalt and Pudder get into an Elevator on the other side of a large 40 sub-level gap in the city scape. The elevator doors close and Cobalt frantically swats the buttons inside.

Muffins and Oscar see him in the elevator across the gap! Oscar says, "He's already getting away!"

"So am I." Muffins runs and jumps down– 10 levels of cat steps, landing on top of the elevator as it's descending! The elevator touches down to the bottom floor and Muffins jumps down from the elevator car as Cobalt and Pudder come sprinting out of it with no hesitation!

Cobalt runs to a city car parked in a parking garage at that level. He sees the red one, sleek like a sports car, with Shallow putting Dr. Bonkers in the back seat. "This rental is so ugly." Dr. Bonkers says.

Cobalt runs up putting the gun in her face, "Get in the car! Get in the car!" They both get in! He closes the door as Pudder gets inside, puts his paw on the ignition and the car starts!

"I need to go to the bathroom." Dr. Bonkers says.

Suddenly bullets blow holes in the window and ricochet off the metal! Cobalt backs up quickly and hits Muffins with the car and Muffins is tossed up spinning in the air, landing on his feet! Cobalt's taking off, Muffins thinks quickly and looks to the car that was parked next to that one, the Purple average looking car!

Just then, Shallow appears onto the road with Dr. Bonkers in the back seat and Cobalt driving and Pudder in the front, being followed by Calico Gang members in other stolen vehicles! "It's Shallow!" Oscar yells. Muffins comes flyin' out of the parking garage in a purple car chasing behind Cobalt in the red sports car. Muffins pulls over for Oscar to get in and they take off down the road after Cobalt and Pudder who have now gotten much further ahead of them! Muffins yells at him, "They're getting away now! Thank myow for holding me back!"

Suddenly the Calicos are just behind them in black cars firing machine guns like crazy at them. "What's going on?" Oscar asks, "They're after them too!"

"They're chasing both of us!" Muffins says!

Guns fire off back and forth putting holes in the sides of the cars! Oscar holds his badge out the window screaming, "Space Police!"

"Shoot him!" Muffins yells!

Oscar points his gun over and starts tagging up the car with bullets- the car loses control and slams into the back of a parked car, exploding ito a ball of flames! The Red car ahead blows out the back windows with their guns and start firing back at Oscar and Muffins with Shallow crouched down- her paws over her ears inside!

Cobalt drives the red car into an active intersection with crossing traffic and a red light. Shallow braces for impact as the red car slams into the side of a freight truck and several cars on the road smash into the back end of the crash! Muffins swerves around the crash quickly and pulls over to a dead stop on the side of the road as all the Calico gang's cars and other public cats cars smash into this pile up.

"I need to go to the bathroom." Dr. Bonkers says.

Muffins screeches the wheels and does a full 180 degree turn and storming off down the road at the crash as the calico cats are getting out quickly with their machine guns drawn. Muffins drives by as Oscar fires his gun off wildly blowing arms and heads off the Calico cats, painting the street red in cat's blood!

Suddenly the Pussy Patrol shows up

in their turquoise Pussy Patrol Vehicles! They stop, get out abruptly, and use their car doors as shields while in the middle of a sudden shoot out! Muffins jumps out the side of the car and start firing off bullets at the gang as machine guns are going off left and right! The streets spark with scraped metal flash, putting tiny potholes in! Gunshots flare across the top of Pussy Patrol units and the cats get down abruptly!

"What the myowk is this?" Oscar says, "Ms. Twinkle Toes says we don't need the back up and now all of the sudden… we need the back up!"

Shallow somehow manages to Swat Pudder in the face, and take Cobalt's gun away, putting it to his head, "Keep drivin'," she says.

"I need to go to the bathroom." Dr. Bonkers says.

The Red car, with what it had left in it, drove forward away from the smashed cars and shootout madness behind it!

Pussy Patrol Unit Windows explode as bullet holes polka dot the cars like a cheese grater! The ground pops up all around Oscar and Muffins like a war zone as they exchange more gun fire! The headlights explode and the tire pops! The siren lights smash out like broken bottles! Muffins stands up quickly and fixes his aim on one calico and rapid fires, BAM BAM BAM! The bullets hit the cat's chest and blood spatters everywhere!

The Calicos start firing their weapons at the Red Car, redirecting their attention!

The Pussy patrol move in, and Oscar and Muffins run back up on their Purple car to give chase! The engine revs it's gears on the road as the horizon besides them streak! The Red car is once again, just ahead of them, on a freeway in the city, but suddenly a Freight truck drives onto the freeway and begins tailing the red car, in front of the Purple one with Muffins and Oscar.

The Freight truck bumps a car in front of it on the freeway and demolishes it's back end like tinfoil- sends the car spinning off to the left! Muffins swerves to avoid it, kicking up the dust, as it crashes into the wall! The back doors open on the freight trailer and calico cats with machine guns start firing at the purple car, blowing its head lights out! "Shit!" Muffins yells. Oscar shoots back in response and the truck swerves, sideswiping another pedestrian cat vehicle- crushing it!

Machine guns are firing off everywhere, the Calicos in the back of the trailer release a caster pallet container that falls off the back of the truck and starts bouncing along the traffic hitting more pedestrian cars. The container smashes into a windshield, making the car veer off right smashing into another car, Muffins barely avoiding the hit! They release another one that most cars avoid the second time around as it tumbles down the freeway.

As the freeway begins to turn up the wall towards E Side in the Engine District, *the fold of the taco*; they release a 3rd one from the trailer that's attached to a chain within the trailer, and as the container hits the road, it tugs at the trailer and slows the truck down as the Red car begins to gain distance! Muffins maneuvers the car past the wildly bouncing chained container as it comes down like a spiked ball and chain, and then flies over the top of the car as Muffins swerves left! It smashes into another car and sends it back sideways hitting 2 other Pussy patrol units on the road! "Oh shit!" Oscar yells!

"That will squint myow tail esophagus." Muffins says.

Muffins gets the car up past the truck

and Oscar points his gun out the window on the right side of the car and shoots the engine as it explodes and the vehicle makes a dead halt!

Cobalt pulls off the freeway in the Engine District with a skidding obtuse turn. Muffins trailing behind him; he drives to the end of the block and takes a left quickly, but Muffins cuts across the large open sidewalk corner, over to the street Cobalt turned onto! Muffins rams the back of the red car hard whiplashing them! "It's not enough." Muffins says, and he pulls the car up beside Cobalt on the left and rams his right side into the red car, smashing and scraping up the exterior loudly! Muffins swings the car out and back in, ramming the red car again! The Red car rams back! Muffins rams into the red car again as Cobalt pulls his gun out and shoots back at them over and over! They duck down to avoid getting shot!

Suddenly a 3rd silver car comes in driven by Oreo 7! He swerves right with the front tip of the car hitting the back tip of the red car, forcing it to lose traction, spinning out of control into the wall of a building on the alley side near the opening. It was sitting up on its side with the top against the wall! Muffins screeches to a stop and parks the car quickly; he asks, "Is everyone okay?"

"I need to go to the bathroom." Dr. Bonkers says.

Muffins gets out of the car quickly with Oscar beside him. Oreo7 Steps out of his silver sports car and walks directly over to the Red car on it's side, jumping on top, and pulling Pudder out as Cobalt quickly runs off. Oscar run up on Cobalt, and tackles him and cuffs him. Muffins grabs Pudder away from Oreo and throws him up against the underside of the red car. He Swats him around lightly to get his attention, while Oreo starts going through his pockets. Pudder yells, "Suck my butt!"

"Where is Cataclysma?!" Muffins yells into Pudder's face.

"Get mauled by a dog." Pudder says defiantly. Shallow is crawling out of the top of the car as it all happens.

"Let me see," Muffins says as he picks the cat up and holds him against the hot engine making Pudder scream uncontrollably! Muffins pulls him off the burn with Oreo 7 still flipping through little photos and cards in the cat's wallet, "Let me see what myow love more, myow vanity or myow life!"

"If myow kill me, myow'll never

find Cataclysma!" Pudder yells, again, defiantly.

"Where is he?" Muffins asks again.

"He's here!" Pudder says, "But myow don't know where! I could show myow!"

Muffins reals it back in, and Oreo gives Pudder back his wallet and things from his pocket. Oreo says, "Myow I.D. photo looks distasteful. There's probably nothing myow can do about it."

"You are a loser." Muffins says.

Oreo greets Muffins, "Good show."

Muffins shakes paws with him, "Yeah, I know."

"Is this How myow do things?" Shallow asked unimpressed and almost insulted by it, "Myow just walk up into a place and hold myow guns out and tell everyone to stop, like that's not a hypocrisy; like that's the solution to creating justice in the Galaxy?"

Muffins thinks a moment, and decides, "Yes."

"Yes?! Yes?!" Shallow's mind is blown and she freaks out, "Oh my Hands! Oh my Hands!"

She meow-screams and Dr. Bonkers yells aggressively still stuck inside the car tipped up on its side, "SHUT UP!"

Oreo 7 says optimistically, "At least they won't be using Catnip flavored Chicken-breasts to finance revolutions."

"I might kiss myow." Oscar says to Shallow.

"What?" she was caught totally of guard as the timing was sudden and awkward.

"Yeah. It could happen right now." He says to her.

"What if I'm a bad kisser?" she asks.

"That's impossible," Oscar says, "unless myow're swishing nova cane."

He goes in for a kiss and it's a light soft kiss. He keeps his face close to her as she looks away and he says, "Okay, maybe myow need to work on it a little bit."

"I went." Dr. Bonkers says.

7 ● PARASITES

The PSPSPS (*Protective Space Police Station Patrol Ship*) has finally reached a 40 yard proximity to the SS Pussy Willow, and the Special Team has returned to impound and jail both Pudder and Cobalt, along with several Calico gang members still jailed away on the SS Pussy Willow. The Pirate Ship is still at bay just yards away from the bottom of the Taco side of the SS Pussy Willow near the Pussy Port. Oscar, Shallow, Muffins, Oreo and Dr. Bonkers are around the table in the conference room with Ms. Twinkle Toes. They're reviewing surveillance tapes of the event that took place in the middle of the city of the SS Pussy Willow. Oscar says, "I don't think it was supposed to be this easy to catch these guys. Something's fishy."

"What do myow mean, myow just chased them all over 'B Side', in the Puss City." Oreo 7 says.

"Yeah but like, when we arrived, Pudder and Cobalt started running while everyone else was like… continuing the loot," Oscar says, "They just got up and ran, kay? There was no challenge or rebellion or defiance, it was just up and run."

"Don't focus on their schemes," Dr. Bonkers says, "focus on getting more information. These guys are a bunch of big dumb muscles."

"I resemble that remark!" Muffins says.

"Yeah, I know!" Bonkers replies.

Muffins reiterates, "Careful how myow talk around me. Muscular people are the reason myow are capable of things bigger than myowself."

"He's caused the death of 34 cats in 24 hours." Shallow says.

"Everybody's different." Muffins says.

"Here's the real question," Dr. Bonkers asks, "Why do they need Cataclysma if they're the ones out looting? They can easily take it for themselves."

"Because he makes weapons." Oreo 7 says, speaking up over them finally. Everyone waited a moment while he confidently spoke on, "Cataclysma is after something else. But so long as he provides weapons to Mr. Bigglesworth, the Calico Gang can raid the Taco shaped SS Pussy Willow."

Bonkers says, "That still doesn't explain why he takes credit for the crimes, when other gangs are pursuing them. Why does he need a Power source?"

"That's a good question," Oreo says.

"It is?" Muffins asks.

"By the way," Oreo 7 says to Bonkers still breathing heavy and crazy behind the face guard, "Myow work on the art of reason is a masterpiece, myow deserve a whole week at the Pussy house. I'm also a huge fan of myow being insane, it's a sure sign of myow genius, an artifact of my ego when I have guests over for parties."

"Thanks." Bonkers says reluctantly.

"Dr. Bonkers," Ms. Twinkle Toes wanted to remind, "is here on permit. After this investigation is over, he will be returned to solitary confinement. He is strictly here to help us track down Cataclysma. Nothing more."

Shallow walks into an interrogation room with Pudder sitting in the seat behind the table, laughing.

"What's so funny?" Shallow asks.

"Myow've fallen right into the trap of Maximus. He wanted us in here." Pudder says.

"Then why did myow give such good chase?" Shallow asks.

"Fake it til myow make it." He says.

"Myow think myow're so clever-"

"-I know I'm clever-"

"-but myow're not-"

"-very clever-"

"-Myow're just a stupid cat."

"Am I?" Pudder asks, "It's only a matter of time before our plans succeed and this entire space station is completely destroyed."

"How do myow think myow can do that?" she asks.

"That's the best part," Pudder smiles sinisterly, "why do anything, when myow have a monster among myow own team?"

She looks at him quickly caught and annoyed, at a loss for words. She paces and then asks, "Is that how myow plan to spend the rest of myow life?" and walks out. "Okay Mother." Pudder says.

In the Jail of the PSPSPS, the criminal cats jailed in there are in the cafeteria portion of the jail. Yellow eyes watch from the dark shadowy corner of the room while everyone is eating, and the tables are serious. No one is happy. Pudder looks around at all the garbage these cats have to eat in here and says, "The first thing I'm going to do when I get out of this place is get some decent food."

"Well myow eat the stuff like it's myowking delicious." Cobalt says. "I'd rather be eatin' something else right now, but I don't see any bitches in here."

Everyone laughs a little and Pudder starts coughing. "What's the matter?" Cobalt says, "The food is too spicy?" but Pudder continued to cough. Suddenly he fell back in convulsions on the floor, and Cobalt spread everyone back away from him, "Don't touch him! Don't touch him!"

Suddenly Pudder starts screaming in agony as blood starts spewing out of the cat's butt hole all over the tile floor! The Cats scramble away meowing like crazy! A bump formed and squeezed out of the cat's butt hole pinch to expose a massive Tapeworm looking around at everyone and examining the room! The alarms blare with red lights flashing as Pudder is laying on the ground unconscious! The Tapeworm crawls back into Pudder's butt hole, and Pudder comes to… as if to wake from a nap. The rest of the cats are staring at Pudder with absolute terror. Pudder sits down at the cafeteria table and continues to eat as he says, "Geez, this food needs more flavor."

Just then, the Space Police Biohazard Unit, *a Chartreux cat named Rocky and an American Shorthair name Pepper cat*, comes in and Fires a gun at Pudder's head, with blood slashing out his ear, he drops with his food to his face on the table. The Tapeworm spews out of Pudder's butt hole again and squirms on the ground towards the Space Police as they fire their guns at it over and over but it slithers away quickly into a nearby ventilation shaft!

"Why would myow do that?" Cobalt yells at them, "He was alive!"

"He's been dead," the Space Cop Pepper says, lighting up a smoke and taking a breath of it, blowing it our, "There's no telling for how long the Tapeworm had been puppeting Pudder, but it's clear…" He takes another drag, "Pudder…" and blows it out, "…putted a foul."

"Bad news." Ms. Twinkle Toes reports to the group in the Conference.

"What is it?" Shallow asks,

"They have tapeworms." Twinkle Toes says.

"What do myow mean they have tapeworms?" Muffin asks.

"I mean they have the big ones," Ms. Twinkle Toes insists, "the ones that splash out of myow butt hole."

"How do myow know?" Oscar asks.

"Pudder's butt hole's been splashed." Twinkle Toes says, "It's only a matter of time before Cobalt's butt hole gets splashed as well. That means everybody on the pirate ship has tapeworms that will eventually splash out of their butt holes."

"Stop saying splash!" Bonkers complains, "Myow make it sound sOoo *wet*!"

"What are we gonna do?" Oscar asks.

Muffins insists, "If it bleeds, we can bleed it out slowly until it dies."

Oreo says, "We need to warn the SS Pussy Willow!"

Behind glass, Cobalt is in an interrogation room with one-way mirror windows. Oscar says to him over the microphone, looking at him through the glass, "So listen dude, myow're infected with a Tapeworm Parasite that's going to eventually splash out of myow butt hole."

"How do myow know that?!" Cobalt yells at the mirror, "Just because he had a Tapeworm doesn't mean we all have Tapeworms!"

"These are no ordinary Tapeworms, bruh." Oscar says calmly, trying to level with him, "These are a different kind of Tapeworm, bruh. They don't just hangout in myow tummy eating myow num-nums all day, these things will inevitably, without a doubt, in 100% fact, knowing the future with certainty and calculation, that a Tapeworm *WILL splash...* out of myow butt hole."

Cobalt suddenly felt the panic, "No! Myow're lying!"

"I'm telling myow the truth." Oscar says. "And if that's true, the only way myow could've gotten the parasite is from Maximus Cataclysma!"

"Why would he do that?"

"To cover his tracks, bruh." Oscar says like a creepy convincing cop, "That's all it takes in this space age of cats. Myow just hire some mother myowkers, give em'

Tapeworms, they give myow what myow hired them to give myow and then they leave with Tapeworms splashing out of their butt holes and no one hears from them again, …it's the perfect crime. Silence the voices of myow temporary allies."

"That doesn't make any sense!" Cobalt yells, "Then why is Pudder dead?"

"What does that matter?"

"He was Max's representative! Myow didn't know that? Why would he want to kill his own? That's counter-productive to his income!"

"Then it was Mr. Bigglesworth." Oscar says.

Cobalt thought about it a moment, "…maybe, But I'm NOT Buyin' it easily! It's gotta be difficult!"

"Either way," Oscar says with a hard Surfer curl in his words, "myow friend let a Tapeworm run loose on this myowkin' *SHIP*, Cobalt! Endangering the lives of an entire intellectual population of *CATS*! …Myow're myowkin' *UP* right now!"

"I didn't let lose Tapeworms!" Cobalt defends, "They came out of Pudder's butt hole!"

"Yeah, but myow came from the same infected ship!" Oscar reasons.

"So what, is this guilty by association?"

There's a silence in the room… and then Oscar says… "myowkin' A it is."

8 ● FALLING SKIES

"What are myow doing, Oreo 7?" Ms. Twinkle Toes asks, walking into the Conference room starkly.

"I've been wondering similar things about myowself." Oreo says.

"Myow're supposed to be locating Cataclysma." She says, "Why are myow just sitting here?"

Dr. Bonkers insists, "We need more information to draw a conclusion. We should be putting the Pirate Ship under siege."

"What do myow plan to do with Cataclysma once myow've caught him?" Oreo asks, "This is the most notorious criminal mastermind in the galaxy."

Just then, Oscar walks into the room, "I don't know what they're planning to do, but I know the Space Police and Cataclysma have had a past working together."

Twinkle Toes defends, "Those are just negative perspectives of a time when we had different associations-"

Oreo 7 pulls up a holographic image of a contract signed between the PSPSPS and Cataclysma "-I beg myow pardon- what's this?"

Shallow and Muffins walk into the conference room overhearing the conversation down the hall. Yellow eyes spy on them in the dark shadows. Shallow looks over to Dr. Bonkers, and begins to truck him forward out of the room, but he hammers the breaks and stops the dolly in the middle of the room, "Did *MYOW* know about this?"

"Cataclysma manipulated myow," Shallow says, "myow're not here because of me."

"I want to know why the Space Police had a contract with Cataclysma." Dr. Bonkers insists.

"Because we didn't know he was evil then." Ms. Twinkle Toes says, her memories reverb back to the times had, "We were protecting the Chickenian planet from a Snakian Invasion! They were steeling eggs and eating chickens whole! It was outrageous, but suddenly Maximus Cataclymsa came into the picture and brought all the resources needed to kick the Snakians out! So, we intercepted, and war broke out between the Catians and Snakians and the Catians of course won after several snake bites and clawing the myowk out of snakes like window drapes and couches. If it wasn't for Cataclysma, we wouldn't have won that war... but we would soon after... discover that Cataclysma was the very source of power that sent the Snakians to invade the Chikenian Planet to begin with, and we have been after Cataclymsa ever since– we closed the contract."

"Or did myow?" Dr. Bonkers assumes with a devious giggle.

"The buck doesn't stop there," Toes continues, "we've become the Space Police we are today because the Galaxy is filling up with forces that are greater than Piracy or Terrorism, it's outright Special Tyranny. We are prepared to deal with those things and control them."

"Like myow controlled Cataclysma?" Oscar asks.

Muffins interjects, "myow work with Cataclysma is what brought Mr. Bigglesworth's Space Pirate Ship to the SS Pussy Willow Intergalactic Taco Space City in the first place; it's a sign to all the other scum in space that the Catians are becoming a volatile species, and that we're ready to be looted like a bunch of pussies."

"Ready to be looted?" Oscar asks.

Ms. Twinkle Toes continues, "We

have to be prepared to deal with all scenarios so we're showing off to intimidate the other races."

"By creating the very Villain we'd never wanted to exist." Oreo says.

"Myow wouldn't even be here if there wasn't a problem," Twinkle Toes brushes him off.

"I thought we were better than this!" Muffins demands.

"Do myow think the Space Police would function better under myow command, Muffins?" Twinkle Toes asks brashly.

"Are myow all blind, def and dumb?" Shallow yells, "The Space Police is designed to handle these threats or else there wouldn't be a Space Police!"

"So everyone in the Galaxy is threatened all the time." Dr. Bonkers says, "Got a pack of coyotes in the bushes while I'm out camping next to the fire with a shotgun!"

The Yellow Eyes exit the room through the shadows as the team continues to banter at each other in disagreement. As the yellow eyes creep along corridors, the dark eventually falls on the master control room to the PSPSPS. The Yellow eyes wander the dark shadows inside the room.

Suddenly, stepping out of the shadows… is *the Black Cat,* 'Shadow', Cataclysma's Assassin. He Swats up the two cats at the helm of the ship over and over SWAT! SWAT SWAT! SWAT SWAT SWAT SWAT SWAT SWAT! SWAT SWAT SWAT!- subduing them, as the crew below seemed to continue working without noticing Shadow.

Suddenly in the corner of his eye, he noticed something rather particular; **a full glass of water sits on a table next to the controls** and Shadow stands there staring at it. It was as if the Glass of water was staring back at him, but no… it can't be… it was just Shadow… it was just an illusion, but no… it doesn't matter anymore. The glass of water sat on the table and Shadow kept looking at it with his black tail gently waving back and forth. Suddenly, one of the crew members below looks up and sees Shadow looking over at the Glass of water. Shadow notices that he's been seen now. He has been seen looking at the glass of water on the table next to the controls. The crew member makes a stern and angry face, telepathically saying to him, "Don't myow mywoking dare." But the desire is too great. Shadow stares back into the crew member's eyes, there eyes locked as he extends his paw. "Don't myow myowking dare." The crewcat shook his head with his paw up to his neck and acted as if he'd cut throat, but Shadow's tension only grew as his paw came closer.

"Intruder!" the crew member yells, and Shadow tips the glass of water over spilling it onto the controls as electricity fries across the board sparking a fire and putting the lights out on the deck! Meows, screeching and hissing everywhere! The only thing that could be seen is Shadow's yellow slit eyes, closing into the dark! The ship's Alarm starts to whale as red lights flash and Cats are running around spasmodically and hysterical! The Entire Space Station docked 40 yards away from the SS Pussy Willow, suddenly starts moving forward towards the SS Pussy Willow! 39 ½ yards… 39 yards… 38 ¾ yards… 38 ½ yards…. The Cats break into the main control room deck where Shadow was, waving around flashlights frantically trying to figure out a solution!

In the Conference room, the Gravity

suddenly shut off, and everyone was floating free as the lights go out throughout the entire ship. They were as if silhouettes over the canvas of the blue gas planet and the oncoming Massive Taco! The lights suddenly came back on hooking into a backup generator, and the Gravity turns back on as everyone drops to the ground!

"Time to get to work." Oscar says to Oreo as he gets up and runs out the door with Muffins right behind him.

The Entire Station is in panic mode as S.W.A.T. Cats are taking positions at certain areas and the rest of the cats are running up and down hallways screaming with no destination! The Entire ship moves closer to the SS Pussy Willow, but moving closer towards the planet and away from the massive Taco, as the tip top of the PSPSPS hits the bottom edge of the SS Pussy Willow and nudges it into a slight snail slow spin! The PSPSPS descends towards the Blue Gas Planet!

"Give me status!" Ms. Twinkle Toes says on her intercom.

'Gizmo', the Norwegian Forest Cat, is the Engineer on the PSPSPS and he speaks back on the intercom, "The entire control system is fried! We need to override it from another location!"

The crew member next to him make a dire look, "Sir, the only other location to control the ship from is the industrial control station at the opposite end of the box!" That was in a location in the corner of the box where there was glass on all three sides, which meant, in order to get there, "We need to hurry!"

Oscar and Muffins arrive at the control deck and Gizmo runs over to them, "We need to get to the Industrial Control Station!"

"Where is it?" Muffins asks. Gizmo points out the window at the box at the other end of the ship corner away from the city side of the ship. Muffins says, "Follow me."

"No, I'll handle it with Oscar," Oreo 7 says to Muffins suddenly arriving, "myow need to find Dr. Bonkers."

"What do myow mean?" Oscar asks.

"Well," Oreo says, "After the lights went out and the gravity misbehaved-"

Muffins rolls his eyes and has a fit, "Stupid psychopaths! Always myowkin' up what's already myowked up!"

They all run in their respective directions to tackle the problems!

Shallow is searching the entire room as the dolly and face guard are lying on the floor, she goes running out of the room, And sees, "Dr. Tiger!" she says surprised.

"Shallow!" he says equally surprised, "C'mon! We need to panic!"

"No!" She yells, "I need to find Dr. Bonkers!"

"Shallow," he says, "I hear something…"

Suddenly from around the corner in the hall, Dr. Bonkers wearing the cut-off fuzzy face of another cat comes around the corner with a chainsaw and starts slashing Dr. Tiger as Shallow screams in a terrifying meow being traumatized! Blood sprays everywhere! The hallway is a red mess of fuzzy guts and Shallow loses her mind with fear, running away immediately as the lights go out again! Dr. Bonkers goes running after! She runs aimlessly down the hall feeling around with her paws, shaking like a freezing cold kitten in the dark!

She runs up to a point in the hall where filing cabinets had fallen over and blocked the path- she runs into them not seeing them and falls over the cabinet in the dark. AS she was tripping over and tumbling down the hall, Dr. Bonkers walks up on the cabinets and steps over them carefully.

Suddenly Shallow finds herself cornered at a dead end of the hallway as Dr. Bonkers revs up the chainsaw from the other end in the dark, she screams out of her mind with her paws to her head and opens the nearest door that goes into a room, opening the door quickly, going in, slamming it shut behind her and locking it! Suddenly the Chainsaw rips through the door, cutting a ragged line across the door into the wall as Shallow meow-screams insanity bouncing around the room like a rodent on fire! The Chainsaw stabs into the wall again Xing the first line towards the top of the cut while Shallow scratches at the walls insanely! She sees the closet and notices the space suits with mobility jet packs! The Chainsaw finished ripping a second line and Shallow runs to the closet, quickly getting into a space suit! The chainsaw stabs into the wall again, as it appears Dr. Bonkers is cutting a triangular hole in the wall and door! Half way through cutting, the wall portion falls off and he stops… just to look through the hole and see her in there… but he didn't see her. He revs the Chainsaw again and finished the final cut as Shallow is in the space suit lighting up.

Holding a rope tied around her wrist and held in her paw, she jumps towards the window placing the barrel tip of an 'Omega Pulse Gun' to it and pulling the trigger! One shot fired, the wave moved out from the center like a water drop hitting a body of calm water, causing the window the explode out and sucks both Dr. Bonkers and Shallow out of the room into the open of the Glass Box Space Station. She looks back and meow-screams out of her mind inside her bubble helmet; he's just feet behind her! Both of them are at the distance of about 4 feet, unable to reach each other, floating uncontrollably forward towards the glass wall with nothing but absolute vibrant lit blue of the gas giant beyond that.

She tries to use the jet pack on the suit but the battery is dead! She panics! Of course, inside the oxygen-filled Glass Box Space Station, several corndog shuttles, satellites, and other contraptions are floating inside like a traffic formation. One of the satellites flashing green and blue is slowly floating into her direction! The Closer she gets to it, the bigger it becomes, until she meets with it, and it's the size of a small house. She grabs it with her tightest paw grip, and holds on dearly. The Satellite continues to pass in its destination as Dr. Bonkers was creeping towards it as well! She meow-screams terrified and frantically looks for a way to get into the Satellite but it's locked in! She starts crawling around it like the edge of a building on a planet with no gravity, and Dr. Bonkers makes contact with the Satellite just around the corner of the box shape from her. He puts both paws up above him with his feet locked onto the Satellite and revs up the chainsaw loudly like a sick twisted victory ceremony while she meow-screams bloody murder! She somehow opens a door into the satellite and launches herself into it, slamming the door shut, locking it, deadbolting in, and meow-screaming in the same breath!

She screams into the radio, "HELP ME! HELP!!!" as she meow-screams insanity! She floats weightlessly up a duct of stairs in the Satellite when suddenly the chainsaw tip stabs in between the door-cutting off the deadbolt and latches! The Door swings open! She screams like she's already being stabbed even though she's just a dumb cat, hysterically twitches uncontrollably, Gets to the other end of the

Satellite, unlocks the other door, and projectiles herself out of it towards the City portion of the Space Police Station! Dr. Bonkers sees her move and jumps at the opening, grabbing the edge while there with the chainsaw in his other paw cutting sparks along everything he accidentally hit. He then jumps at her, behind her, with a harder thrust than her, catching up to her! Slowly creeping up, she sees him behind her and starts meow-screaming again! 9 feet away… 8 feet away… 7 feet away… 6 feet away… 5 feet away… 4 feet away… she was getting closer to a building and was beginning to feel the pull of the artificial gravity. She cruised closer and her paw touched a garage door on the building side- she grabbed a handle on it with both paws as Dr. Bonkers floated close quick! She meow screams, "Oh no! NO! NO NO!"- the door begins to open and Dr. Bonkers swings the Chainsaw at her but he's just a hair too far away as he floats past and the garage door pulls her up! She grabs onto the inside of the door and starts crawling in until the artificial gravity pulls her down to the floor- and then she runs towards the door and sees Muffins behind the glass! "Muffins!"

"What is going on?" he asks.

"Dr. Bonkers is loose!" she yells, "He's trying to kill me!"

"Good," he says, "now I have a reason to kill him." He puts on a Space Suit and opens the door, letting Shallow in and trading her places.

"But he has a chainsaw!" she yells!

"My red rocket is so hard it'll grind his chainsaw teeth down." He says, and turns around, going out the door, "I'll be back when I feel like it." The door closes behind him, and they're separated by glass.

Ms. Twinkle Toes is on the deck of the ship waiting to hear back from Oreo, Gizmo and Oscar at the other end of the Mother Ship. Oscar says over the Radio, "We're in the Control room."

"Great," Ms. Twinkle Toes says, "Now we just need myow to reboot the system so that it will redirect the controls to the uppermost primary control center, which should lead back here!"

Inside the Deck, Oscar, Gizmo and Oreo are wearing Space Police Suits with flashlights looking around in the darkness. Oscar radios, "Copy."

Gizmo walks over to the main control panel and says, "This is the one, we just need to do a hard reboot."

"Myow know how to do that?"

"Yes." Gizmo says. He presses a few buttons and the screens boot up with an image of a slice of pink and white cake with a rainbow behind it. Then it switches to a screen that says, "System Rebooted."

"So that's it?" Oreo asks.

"Yes." Gizmo says.

"See!" Oscar points at Orco, "Myow're myowking bored!"

The Police Space Station is now stable and floating just 80 miles below the SS Pussy Willow, now closer to the blue gas giant. Ms. Twinkle Toes works frantically with the crew as the system is now back up and running again, "We're up!" she says! But just then, the main door to the control deck opens, and a bunch of Tapeworms start crawling into the room! All the Cats freak-out and turn around hissing and groaning at the Tapeworms as they start firing their guns at them! Ms. Twinkle Toes pulls out a Pistol from her right side and starts firing at the heads of the Tapeworms, popping them open with purple oozing all over the floor when they hit down with a splat! "There's too many of them!" Ms. Twinkle Toes yells!

Dr. Bonkers floats over to another door to get into the building and opens it, getting inside. Muffins watches intently as the door shuts and Muffins floats over to the door. He opens it and sees Bonkers outside the glass of decompression room door ahead running down the hall with the chainsaw turned off in his left paw. Muffins gets the door shut and the room decompresses a moment, allowing him into the building. He goes running down the hall after him and turns the corner, watching Bonkers get into an escape pod! Muffins runs over to him, ready to grab him, reaching in, as Bonkers grabs Muffins in return and yanks him into the escape pod and jumping out! He slams the door shut- pressing the button on the wall, and the deploying the escape pod! It fires out into the Glass Box and joins a line of other Pods, that by now, looking at them from the outside… all look like stacks of Pop Tarts. Muffins looks at the screen inside the pod and sees that they are programmed to leave the PSPSPS in an orderly fashion, to the SS Pussy Willow. "That mother myowker!" Muffins says sternly. Muffins, already wearing the Space suit with fully charged jet pack, hits an emergency release button. The entire Pop Tart Stack Escape pod inside lights up red. Another button appears under the release button that says "confirm" on it. Muffins slams his paw on the button, and the floor of the pod bottoms out, flushing Muffins back out into the Glass Box! He shoves off the Pop Tart Pod and propels his body back towards the city side of the Space Police Station.

Inside the Escape hall, Dr. Bonkers is walking back when a voice says to him from over the intercom, "Myow're a loser waiting to happen." It stops Dr. Bonkers, as he wonders where the voice is coming from, or who's voice it is.

Bonkers says, "'Hope' is a good movie. myow Big bad ass Police Station is falling out of the sky into a massive ball of blue death so, what is my disadvantage here, really? …I mean… let us be serious here… what is it?"

The voice over the Intercom says, "Myow lack grace."

Dr. Bonkers gets into the Escape pod, looking out at the room one last time to say, "Myow lack a face," before closing the pod door.

Cobalt somehow got out of the interrogation room, a lot of criminals that were originally jailed are running free inside lockdown floor but Cobalt was in the interrogation room. He was jogging down the halls as the red lights flash and alarms blare. Then, Shallow spotted him and goes running after him! He's quick- he hears her gallop- turns immediately and Swats her in the face- but she lands on her feet!

They stop in the hallway and groan at each other as they engage in a deadly stare down. Shallow's tail flickers as she groans at him, "Myow're supposed to be in the interrogation room."

Cobalt groans back, "I am the interrogation room."

"What the myowk does that mean?" Shallow asks and Cobalt jumps at Shallow as they sort of jump together in defiance of each other and Cobalt grabs a bite of Shallow's neck and holds her down while she claws at his belly with her back feet repeatedly! She Swats her back foot claws across Cobalt's face as he meow-screams and bites her face with a vice grip! Cobalt Twists around to get on his feet while she's on her back flinging her back feet claws at him as he holds her down by the face! Shallow Back foot claw-swats Cobalt in the face again, and He lets go as they back away from each other quickly and continue to stare each other down. Cobalt panting with his tongue sticking out while Shallow's nose is bleeding, he put his snout up close to her with a little sniff and says, "I'm so glad myow could get a taste of my bang tang."

Shallow swats him, and Cobalt jumps and attacks her as they roll into a ball that wildly flails up and down across the hallway back and forth insanely! Again, her back to the floor, she reaches up and swats the myowk out of his face with her left paw and Cobalt Swats her in the face back, SWAT! SWAT! SWAT! They retract from each other and then she attacks him, shoulder to shoulder, with their bodies twisting left and right attempting to bite each other! There's no penetration!

They both stop to take a breath as blood runs down Shallow's face and snout. Cobalt pants with his tongue sticking out, "I know myow're into me," he says to her, "It'll all make sense once I'm into myow."

She grab him by the head and slams it into the wall completely dazing him with a quick head shake twitch and stars as he tries to get back up but falls back and lays on the floor dizzy. "Mrew…"

9 ● DESERTION

Ms. Twinkle Toes rallies up what's left of the team: Oreo 7 the manx tuxedo cat, Oscar the orange tabby, Shallow the British blue cat and Muffins the maine coon cat. Cobalt the Russian blue cat is in cuffs and being taken with them. They're in the halls of the PSPSPS with Singapura Cats in Space Police Suits, and helmets on. One of them holds a radar-like tracking device that's keeping track of where the Tapeworms may be as they navigate the Space Station. They reach a point where they realize they need an arc weld, and the Singapura Cats work at it steadily.

"Why can't we just go back to the Tilapia pad and take the Saucer?" Shallow asks.

"It's been stolen." Ms. Twinkle Toes says. "There's no other way to escape. The last Escape pods are behind a wall that requires careful cutting with an Arc Weld, in order to reach them."

One of them holds an arc weld with a black tint face screen- the blindingly bright light scorching the surface. The Singapura cat with the radar reads… 200 paws as the radar begins to beep.

"Where's that coming from?" Oscar asks.

"It's comin' from behinds us." The Singapura says.

Muffins grabs one of the Singapura Cat's heavy artillery machine guns, "Give me this."

"120 paws… 110 paws…"

"110 what? They might as well be in the room!" Oscar says.

"90 paws…"

"Myow radar's myowkin' up." Muffins complains.

"70…"

"Where the myowk are they?" Oreo says.

"50…"

"That's in the room!" Oscar says.

"Myow read the radar then! Look at it!" the Singapura says. "30!"

Suddenly the floors start to break up and wobble and the cats start jumping around and meow-screaming as Tapeworms start getting inside the Room from under the tiles on the floor! The Tapeworm's flat bodies come up out of the circuit vents from under the tiles like serpents! Muffins starts unloading bullets on them as purple blood splatters all over the walls and the other cats run terrified to the corner of the room meow-screaming chaotically and jumping up mindlessly!

The Singapura cat with the arch weld finally breaks the surface and opens a path to the remaining Escape Pods! They all run in quickly while Muffins is blasting Tapeworms! All the Singapura Cats start unloading their machine guns on the Tapeworms with Muffins, as Purple blood sprays all over the place like a summer day at a water park! Even Oreo 7n and Oscar pull out their Pistols and begin aiming and firing! Suddenly more Tapeworms start flooding up through the floor!

"We got more of them!" Ms. Twinkle Toes holds Shallow behind her and yells at them, "Get in the Pods! Get in the Pods!" when suddenly a Tapeworm comes right up to her as she struggles to get the gun loaded! She meow-screams like she's being murdered, fixes the gun, aims, and Fires! The head of the Tapeworm explodes and the Purple blood of the worm goops up like slime and falls back down splatting all over Ms. Twinkle Toe's face! "Let's go Now! NOW!"

The Singapura Cats form a wall together firing their machine guns off at Tapeworms with Muffins in the middle of them, and they begin backing up to ready their escape into the pods!

Suddenly one of the Tapeworms comes up from the tiles a cat's standing on and grabs one of the Singapura Cats by the head and pulls him over into the vent shaft as the cat meow-screams! The Singapuras freak out and hiss terrified as they fire at the vent shaft insanely killing both the Singapura cat inside and the Tapeworm that took him! "Got it!" one of them confirms!

All the cats take to escape pods quickly, and Muffins runs to the pod his crew is aboard. The door shuts quickly and outside the windows looking into the hall, the Tapeworms slither up and put their suckers on the glass! The cats meow in disgust. The sealed doors close killing the Tapeworms on the windows and the Pop Tart Stack Escape Pod is released into space away from the Glass Cube PSPSPS altogether. It slowly began to migrate towards the SS Pussy Willow, almost a hundred yards away.

"We were the last to escape." Ms. Twinkle Toes says, "The Space Police

Station is completely Destroyed, Dr. Bonkers is on the loose on the SS Pussy Willow somewhere and it's all because of Maximus Cataclysma. It's a big loss. Myow never see the big loss coming. Yes, it's true we were going to build a foundation with Cataclysma, but that's *been* over, for years. Even then, I never believed in it because I was planning on something more complex. I was planning on something Called the 'Extra Pussies'… because yes… they are Space Police Cats… but they're… something 'Extra'. I was planning to bring together a group of these Cats with special talents… to see if they could become a force more powerful than just 1 pussy; see if they could get the job done when other pussies couldn't; to battle those dickheads out there that other pussies were too weak to handle." She looks over at Shallow and says, "Dr. Tiger died believing in it, or else Dr. Bonkers wouldn't have helped us this far." There's a silence, as the cats all seemed stressed and beat.

"So like, does that mean we get to myowk em' up, neow?" Oscar asks.

She hesitates… "Yes."

At the SS Pussy Willow, the Escape Pod is lined up and received at the Pussy Port. The Extra Pussies step out of the Pop Tart Stack Escape Pod onto the deck and walk out to the Pussy Port. They're greeted by Space Police Council-Cat, 'Precious.'

"Greetings fellow Space Police officers." Precious says, "If myow don't mind, the Captains of the SS Pussy Willow are demanding to meet with myow at once."

"Right away, thank myow." Ms. Twinkle Toes says, and she leads the group. They take a short ride transport to a building between the Engine District, and the Pussy Port. They then ride an elevator up the building side, and reach a level that, when the doors open, is very posh, fancy, clean, modern, white and with fur walls. The Captains are inside amongst each other talking when they look over to see the Extra Pussies walking in. Captain Sass, Captain Peyimess and Captain Grafenberg are all ragdoll cats. They're surrounded by security and surveillance equipment, speaking over the situation with Security officer Spike, the Abyssinian.

"Twinkle Toes!" Captain Sass

exclaims, "Don't myow show up in the damnedest places!"

"What is all of this?" Twinkle Toes asks.

"C'mere everyone," Captain Sass waves them over with her paw, "I have something myow might find interesting."

"Have we gained more information on the Pirate Ship?" Oreo 7 asks.

"They're still refusing contact with the SS Pussy Willow." Captain Sass says.

"What is this?" Muffins asks.

"How many times do I have to tell myow," Sass says to Twinkle Toes specifically, "Myow don't know what myow're dealing with." She turns around and presses a button on the dash and the screen plays a surveillance shot of Shadow coming out of the Shadows on the control deck of the PSPSPS and spilling a glass of water on the controls, only before vanishing into the dark again. "Myow see that? There's myow destroyer. He's using Dark technology, the only way to detect him is by butt hole smell signature. 10 years ago this same assassin destroyed an entire elite forces unit with the Space Police on a Planet somewhere else. There were only 2 survivors, and they said he has the ability to travel through shadows and darkness. It's Dark technology, the kind of stuff that our current science can't explain."

"Where did he get it?" Shallow asks.

"Some are suggesting it's Octopusian." Captain Sass says, "How he obtained the technology is unknown."

"Wrong again myow dumb pussies!" Shadow says from the door of the room holding a fully automatic machine gun that he'd obviously stolen from a Singapura Cat! Everyone's frozen as he chuckles a little, "Octopusian? Geez, myowk those guys. I can't even eat them without spitting them out and coming back later to chew on them again. Why don't we just make gum out of them anyway?"

"How did myow get in here?" Shallow asks.

"You dumb bitch."

"We just talked about it!" Captain Sass paw smacks her forehead.

"Let Cobalt go," Shadow says, "or I'll completely end everything right now."

Ms. Twinkle Toes unlocks the arrest leash and uncuffs Cobalt. Cobalt walks over to the door and walking out as Shadow stares ahead at them, machine gun still drawn, Muffins pulls out his machine gun quickly as the other cats freak out and meow-scream! Muffins pulls the trigger unloading bullets at Shadow! Shadow Fires back with the cats scattering everywhere to take cover! Muffins drives Shadow out the door, and runs to the door to go after Shadow, but as soon as he opens the door, its pitch-black dark.

Outside the building Shadow is looking around everywhere for Cobalt but can't seem to find him among the busy Engine District streets full of industrial worker cats in their grimy work uniforms. His face grows agitated and soon he becomes angry and then furious at the fact that Cobalt pretty much just ditched him!

Inside the white room again, the Captains and the Extra Pussies run to the surveillance screens to see if they can spot Shadow! Spike goes through the cameras looking quickly to find the black cat with yellow eyes! "There he is!" Oscar points with his paw claw hitting the screen, "He's already getting on the Monorail!"

"How do we catch him?" Captain Sass asks.

"Myow don't." Muffins says turning around to walk out the door, "That's my job." He grabs the handle and Oscar runs to join, "I have the radio, keep me updated on where he is at all times until we can catch up with him and stop him."

"Wait," Captain Peyimess stops them and gives them anti-gravity drone back-packs to wear. "Myow'll need these in a city like this."

"Well while myow're doing all of that," Oreo 7 says heading to the door, "I'll be infiltrating the Pirate Ship." Oreo grabs himself his own anti-gravity pack to wear and walks out the door before them.

Spike sees something important and says, "He's on the move! He's getting the gun out and boarding the 'A Side' Monorail!"

10 ● SHADOW CHASE

Shadow quickly pushes other cats aside to board the 'A Side' Monorail and jogs down the hall towards the front of the Monorail where the control station is. He sits in the chair closest to that door and waits patiently, while the cat public was continuing to board the train casually. The doors close as Muffins and Oscar are finally catching up to the Monorail as it's leaving. Muffins and Oscar run at the Monorail still in it's slow and steady acceleration.

"Turn myow pack on." Muffins says as he turns his on and begins to float off the ground and holding the side of the Monorail. Oscar copies his motions and hangs onto the monorail just behind him saying, "Are myow crazy?" The Monorail train gains speed and moves forward swiftly- high speed! Muffins tries to pry the door open and Oscar yells at the window, "Open the door! Open the door!"

The cats on board look at each other carelessly meowing and purring. "We gotta get in this Monorail train!" Muffins says.

"No shit!" Oscar yells at him.

"I have an idea." Muffins says, pulling out a cliff climbing rope and hook and shoving one end in between the door, and then chucking the hook off to catch something. "Heads up."

The rope hooks a building's fire escape's metal frame, and it rips the door right off the side of the Monorail train as the cats inside start meow-screaming and bunching up away from the door blast. Muffins easily crawls in as Oscar is on the side of the Monorail trying to edge towards the door. Muffins Grabs his arm and they jump him into the door, onto the train. The cats cornered up are sitting there watching Oscar and Muffins, "These guys are myowk ups!"

Shadow bolts down the hall of the Monorail at Oscar and Muffins, tackling Oscar in a roll, hitting seats with fur spots blasting up in the claw attacks! Oscar does a flip, lands on his feet and jumps back at Shadow! Oscar grabs shadows head and kicks his hind legs up at shadows chest, with Oscars back facing the ground in his flight! Oscar pounds his claws into Shadow- projecting him to the wall with a hard thud and fall! They stand against each other in a stare down as Muffins watches with his tail wagging knowing that if Oscar doesn't handle him, he was going to without question.

The stare down is deadly as they groan at each other; their eyes cynically slanted. Shadows intimidated by Oscar who doesn't myowk around. Shadow squints and meow-screams at him attempting to swat Oscar but Oscar jumps straight at Shadow, biting his neck to draw blood! They twist and turn rapidly in chaos in wretched cat noises. Chunks of black and orange fur fly around like soap bubbles! Oscar slams Shadow up against the wall and SWAT SWAT SWATs him! Shadow pelts Oscar in the face with his hind paw, smacking Oscar in the nose, busting his lip open! They stare each other down again, looking to kill, Shadow Swat the top of Oscar's head, and Oscar jumps at Shadow again with another wildly twisted turning wrestle of claws, flying fur, and blood drops smearing on the floor and seats!

Shadow goes to run away, but Oscar grabs Shadow by the butt with his claws impaling and pulling his butt back to Oscar-Shadow Hisses viciously and turns swatting Oscar, SWAT, SWAT SWAT! Oscar jumps at Shadow!

Muffins interjects their violent wrestle with his own SWAT SWAT SWAT SWAT, aimlessly just SWATing the fight, SWAT SWAT SWAT SWAT! SWAT SWAT! After a moment they release again, and Oscar cowers with Shadow on his two feet, his other 2 to show dominance. Muffins Swats Shadow, SWAT SWAT SWAT! Shadow Swats him back and then runs off to the Control room through the crowd of cats, forcing the door open, grabbing the machine gun next to the door that he left there, and putting loud holes in the controls as the Monorail begins to accelerate and smoke fills the control room!

Shadow Runs back over to Oscar and Muffins, all three of them look beat to shit, and Shadow takes away Oscar's Anti-Gravity pack at gun point and puts it on, walking over to the door they busted open, and says, "Have fun mother myowkers." Firing the gun at them and jumping out the opened door. Spike says over the radio, "the Monorail is out of control! It can't be stopped. Somebody's gotta stop it!" Oscar and Muffins run to the front end of the Monorail train to the control room and look ahead as they're speeding right through 'Meat Lovers Station' dangerously! Muffins sees them moving along the track that's elevated up towards B Side as it goes in a large Circle like a Cork Screw around buildings that reach from A Side Double Cheese District up into B Side Double Cheese District like one large mass inside the taco. Muffins looks to Oscar, "Is there a way to hold the monorail train on the loop in the 'Double Cheese' district?"

"I don't know." Oscar says, "I've never driven a Taco Space City Monorail train without a control unit before."

"Good." Muffins says, "This life experience will help myow grow as a cat." He turns to the conductor, "Is this the Flop Hop?"

"Yes." The conductor says, "it only has 5 stops between all 3 sides of the Taco Space City."

Muffins says, "Myow mean 5 skips."

"We have to stop soon!" the conductor says terrified, "or we'll run into the back of the monorail train!" -that's currently stopped at the next station! Pussy Patrol Units flashing red and blue lights are speeding towards the next stop the Monorail Train will be racing through on B Side. Captain Sass, Ms. Twinkle Toes, and Shallow are together in a black vehicle that's moving along the public quickly to 'Hawaiian Station'.

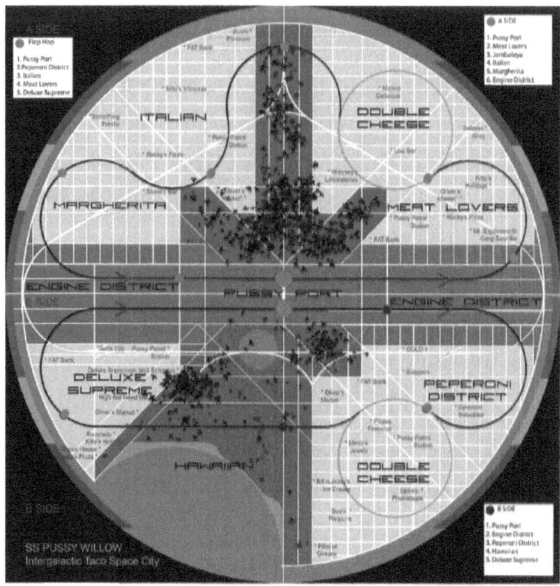

The Station sits right on the park beach side with a road underneath it. The Pussy Patrol units swarm the area with sirens blaring and flashing while cats are running away silently and instantly. They all get out of their vehicles; Shallow runs up ahead of Ms. Twinkle Toes and Captain Sass, as the entire heard of Patrol units moved in unison into the stairwells and up to the platform of the Monorail Station. Shallow gets up to top and runs over to a box on the wall, opening the door lid on it like an electrical main. Ms. Twinkle Toes and Captain Sass reach the top and Toes asks, "Shallow, what are myow doing?"

"Buying time!" she says, as suddenly the monorail train ahead of Oscar and Muffins had already arrived in deceleration along the dock. Shallow looked over and up at the Corkscrew monotrack of Double Cheese, and sees the monorail train coming. As the current monorail train had just stopped, Shallow triggers a spark in the box and caused the track on the dock to switch as the doors on the monorail train open. Everyone was confused. The Monorail with the train on it, moved away from the dock, and another monotrack appeared out from under the dock itself.

"We're not going to make it." Muffins says, "unless we jump off the train before it runs into the next train station." Muffins looks to the conductor, "How much time do we have left to jump?"

"2 minutes!" the conductor says.

"Okay," Muffins says. "Hang in there."

"Wait, what?" the conductor asks, as

Muffins and Oscar leave the control room and start running down the hall while everything outside the windows is flipping from A Side to B Side of the Taco Space City. Muffins and Oscar get to the door and they both look back at all the cats inside the monorail as they all look terrified and Muffins says, "Don't worry, myow'll live through it, it's just going to be a very intense experience for myow, okay. Hang in there." Oscar piggy-backs Muffins, turns on the Anti-Gravity pack, and they both float out the door they busted open. On the outside of the Monorail train, Muffins holds the train in the zero-gravity divide between both A Side and B Side. Muffins speaks into the radio, "where is Shadow now?"

"He's still back on A Side." Spike says.

"I'm on it." Muffins jumps off with Oscar piggy backing, to float down to A Side.

The Monorail train keeps speeding up, barely holding the track as the gravity begins to pull it over to B Side. The G force of the turn tightened more and more, and the cats inside were literally walking quickly around and meowing concernedly on the right ride wall. Just as the track linked into the B Side and is about to complete a turn, the Monorail train begins to set on a right-side angle lean- sparks flying on scraped sides! The monorail train continuing to speed up, the entire monorail train falls over on its right side, shooting off like a rocket through buildings and into the park; crashing into smoke and flames! The cats inside jump out meowing wildly and running away so fast, that we can all rest assured, it wasn't that big of a deal after all, since the monorail train cars were now completely empty! The Pussy Patrol and Fire Units immediately respond to put out the flames!

Muffins gets on the radio as Oscar is still piggy-back, "Where is he?"

Spike says over the radio, "He just got on the freeway headed towards the Jambalaya."

"I see him." Muffins says as they float down towards the Jambalaya Freeway triangle between Double Cheese and Italian. They land on top of a car and Muffins rips the sun-roof open. Oscar gets in, making the cat driving get in the passenger seat, "Hey! Hey! Hey! HEY! What-the! What are myow doing! This is my car!" Muffins gets in second and pushes the driver into the back seat, "What the myowk?"

"We'll give it back, later." Muffins says.

In the car next to them, unbeknownst to them, Whiskers and Lucky are driving in a chromatic purple and green car. Lucky says, "Hey, aren't those the cats that are with the Space Police?" Whiskers nods and calls it in.

"Mr. Bigglesworth. The Space Cops are on the Pussy Willow freeway." Whiskers says.

"What do myow think they're doing?" Mr. Bigglesworth asks over the radio.

"I think they're following Shadow." Whiskers says, "He's on his way to the rendezvous point right now."

"That is a serious problem!" Mr. Biggleworth yells.

"I'll take care of them." Whiskers says cynically.

"I want myow to kill them." Mr. Bigglesworth says, "No more games. We need to show them where the line is."

"Yes boss." Whiskers says.

Oscar drives the car fast up the freeway, passing car after car quickly to catch up with Shadow who sees them in the rearview mirror coming in hot. He speeds up knowing it must be them. Behind Muffins and Oscar, Whiskers and Lucky are vigilantly following. Spike radios into Muffins, "Myow've got followers- purple car- just behind myow." Muffins looks back as he sees them open their sunroof and one of them stand out the top with a machine gun.

"Get down!" Muffins yells, as Lucky unloads a machinegun clip at the car- Oscar swerving left and right, slamming into other cat's cars!

Shallow radio's Spike, "Spike come in."

"This is Spike over."

"Spike, it's Shallow. Where is Muffins and Oscar?"

"He's on the Freeway chasing after Shadow," Spike says, "'A Side', Italian."

Shallow puts the radio down and looks up from where she's at in Hawaiian, at the Italian section that was as a ceiling directly above where she stands. She spotted Oscar and Muffin's car swerving on the freeway like tiny rodents. They could barely be seen standing. Shallow radios, "I'm on my way," running to the black car. Captain Sass and Ms. Twinkle Toes watch her run away to the black car.

Captain Sass says, "She's tenacious." As the radios in the Pussy Patrol units call in the reckless driving and shots fired on the radio.

On the freeway, Muffins pulls out the machine gun, "I'll use whatever I have left in this baby." He puts the gun out the window and aims at Lucky and pulls the trigger and only 5 bullets fire; it's empty. Done. Lucky continues firing at them, Muffins says, "Just clearing the chamber."

Some bigger trucks are just ahead and Oscar takes on a more aggressive approach weaving between the trucks and using them as walls. Lucky continues to fire at them, the bullets spark across the asphalt. Oscar bobs over a few lanes to cruise up behind a family sized car. Lucky unloads the machine gun on the family car, swiss cheesing the body, popping the tires- the cats jump out of the car instantly in a panic and the family car explodes in motion, slamming into the cars behind it as the Pussy

Patrol dodges the debris from the commotion ahead.

Oscar pulls the car ahead to coast up behind a truck and trailer, using it as a wall again. There's a car up front blocking Oscar from speeding up though, as the car and truck box them in. Whiskers drives up behind them with Lucky out the sunroof and he unloads the guns on the car again, it's a Hollywood miracle these cats aren't shot and the car is still running. Instead of shooting at Oscar, he stops firing altogether, aims carefully at the back of the cat's head driving the car ahead of Oscar's, fires the gun, and blows the cats head off with perfection. That car swerves off to the right and hits the truck. Oscar slams on the brakes, turns left immediately, slams the left side of his car into the wall- the dead cat's car passes by them and back as Oscar punches the gas!

Lucky machine guns down the dead cat's car until it explodes into smithereens and Whiskers drives the car right through the middle of it without a problem. Whiskers races forward to catch up with Oscar as Lucky fires his machine gun at Oscar and Muffins, and while able to kill that cat driver back there with one shot, Lucky can't hit a fur tip on these two cats! "This is pointless!" Lucky throws a fit and chucks the machine gun at the Pussy Patrol chasing them!

Oscar says to Muffins, "Myow're bleeding, cat! I think myow're hit!"

"It's just a slow leak." Muffins says.

Oscar drives up alongside Shadow's right side of his car and Muffins says, "I'll be back when I feel like it." He opens the passenger side door and jumps over to Shadow's driver side window and grabs Shadow- biting his face- impaling Shadow's shoulders with his claws and grabbing on tight as Shadows hisses and spasms rapidly and violently with the car swerving quickly left and right all over the freeway! Muffin's so passionately and violently biting Shadow's face and clawing at him that his body is twisting like a helicopter out the window! He's so pissed off that his fur is fuzzed out like a puffer fish! The Car swerves fiercely, slamming into a car on the right!

Oscar slows down and curbs right to get behind Shadow's car as Whiskers follows and drives up beside Oscar slamming into him and pushing the car over all the way into the wall, slowing both cars!

Shadow slams on the brakes and

Muffins loses his grip as he falls to the road tumbling like a foot ball down the freeway to a stop! Shadow leaves him in the dust! Oscar punches the gas and squeezes out from between Whiskers' car's grip and races forward to Muffins screeching to a halt. Muffins gets in, and They race on after Shadow down the freeway!

Whiskers Speeds up again racing after them as the Pussy Patrol catches up and they speak over the megaphone, "This is the Pussy Patrol! Pull myow car over to the side of the road now!" Whiskers pulls out a paw gun and fires it at the Pussy Patrol car repeatedly! Whisker floors it and gets up along side Oscar's car, pointing his gun at the back tire, and firing, blowing it out! Oscar keeps it steady and speeding! Whiskers veers left into Oscar's car bumping him over a lane! Oscar dips a hard left turn and then hard right slamming into Whiskers, pushing his car over towards the Margherita off ramp, shoving Whiskers and Lucky off the freeway!

Oscar slams the gas again and catches up quickly with Shadow again, coming around him on Shadow's left paw side again, as Muffins opens his passenger side door, Shadow veers at them again,

slamming Muffins' door shut! Muffins grabs
Shadow through both windows with his
impaling claw grip, biting shadow's neck,
shadow turns right, and Muffin's pulls
Shadow out of the car through the driver
side window! Shadow's car drives off
aimlessly decelerating down the freeway,
hitting the freeway wall and scraping along
the side on the way up! Oscar stops the car,
and Muffins Swats Shadow across the face
in the middle of the freeway as all the cars
on the freeway stop and meowing
complaints come from inside! Oscar get out
of the car and faces down Shadow with
Muffins! They groan with a deadly stare
down! Shadows groan is much louder as he
feels the most threatened. Muffins jumps at
Shadow with both paws and swats Shadow's
head like a clap! Shadow hisses on the
defense! Oscar jumps at Shadow and Swats
him in the face over and over, SWAT
SWAT! SWAT! SWAT SWAT! Muffins
grabs Shadow with his claws impaling
Shadow's mane and he tosses Shadow into
the back seat of the car with the original
driver jumping out of the car terrified! Oscar
slams the door shut, and they both get in the
car. Muffins radios in, "We got him." Oscar
back in the driver seat, takes off and the

traffic resumes as normal.

Spike says, "The Dark Tech should be a collar located around his neck. It will be black and hard to see with the naked eye." Muffins reaches back to grab it but Shadow groans and swats Muffins paw away, and Muffins jumps at Shadow as they fight in the back seat, Muffins biting Shadows face and SWAT! SWAT! SWAT! SWAT! Swatting Shadow until he's knocked out in the back with his tongue hanging out. Muffins finds the collar and takes it off Shadow.

The scenery outside the car begins to look odd as the freeway begins to transition from A Side into E Side, like driving straight up a cliff face with no problem. Muffins craws back into the front seat and says, "Alright I've got it. Now what?"

"Now, use it." Spike says.

Suddenly Whiskers gets back on the freeway with Lucky reloading his machine gun standing out the sunroof. Muffins looks over to Oscar and says, "I don't trust myow with taking Shadow to the Pussy Patrol Station to be jailed, because I think I'm stronger and can handle him better than myow, so I'm getting in the back seat and putting on the Dark Technology and wearing my Anti-Gravity Pack, and taking this half eaten over cooked distasteful piece of trash behind bars. As soon as we reach Deluxe Supreme on B Side, myow're going to handle those two mother myowkers back there while I fly away to safety."

"Got it!" Oscar says as Muffins jumps into the back seat and puts on the collar. The scenery outside the window still turns as they continue to 'move up the wall', and 'A Side' is suddenly their ceiling as they drive into 'B Side' in Deluxe Supreme District from 'E Side'. Muffins grabs Shadow still unconscious, and takes Shadow out of the car with him, hovering with his anti-gravity pack out and away towards the Deluxe Supreme Mall.

Suddenly a Gang of 6 Calicos in all black suits riding anti-Gravity Bikes roll up right in front of Muffins, "Aw Shit!" He floats over to the highest level balcony of the Deluxe Supreme Mall and enter into the building with the Calico racing right behind him!

Oscar Flips a U-Turn in the Freeway and starts racing the car against traffic, as Whiskers slings shots past Oscar, and screeches to a dead stop to go after him!

Suddenly 4 Calico Anti-Gravity Bikers come down out of the sky on Oscar, coming up just behind him! Oscar swerves off through traffic, dodging each oncoming car, bike, truck and over to the right side of the Freeway! The Calicos lift up hovering over the cars and ready their guns. One of them just starts firing at Oscar while Oscar lets go of the wheel, and lets the car stray off into traffic! Oscar jumps out the right side of the car onto the top of a car on the opposite lane! The former car crashing into an oncoming truck and the Calico open fire on Oscar. Oscar Fires back in return with his paw gun, as he crawls into the car through the passenger seat window, leaving them behind. The Siberian cat inside hisses and swats Oscar in the face over and over! SWAT! SWAT! SWAT! SWAT!

Inside the 8 level mall, Muffins floats through the door of the 8th level balcony food court holding Shadow still unconscious and goes over the paw-rail and hovering down the center of the mall's levels! The 6 Calicos on Bikes destroy the glass as they come soaring in through shattered glass doors, and over the ledge as well, after Muffins! The whole mall is filled with hissing and meow-screams as the shots go off inside! Muffins gets to the bottom level and touches down to run on his hind legs into a shadow where he uses the collar and becomes so shaded by the dark corner that he disappeared with Shadow in his arms.

The Calicos come out of the Mall firing their weapons at the Pussy Patrol and the Pussy Patrol return fire, putting 4 bullets in one Calico, and blowing the back of another's head out through the eye! The Calicos manage to open fire on the Pussy Patrol unit's engine and it explodes into black smoke that gathers into the Zero-G Divide of the Taco!

Muffins runs out the door with Shadow in his arms! The Pussy Patrol arrest the Calicos at the entrance of the Mall as Muffins runs to their Patrol Car and opens the back seat for arrests and puts Shadow in the back, closing and locking the door. He gets in the car when Shallow runs up and pounds on the glass, "I've been trying to catch up with myow this whole time!"

"Get in the car." Muffins says, as Shallow gets in, "We've been chasing Shadow down, up until now. So, where is the nearest Jail Cell?"

"It's only two blocks from here," Shallow says, "Myow completely passed it coming off the freeway."

"Shut up." Muffins says and he puts the car in reverse, driving off towards the nearest Pussy Patrol Station. The Remaining 4 Calicos are captured by the Pussy Patrol and are taken into custody at the Pussy Patrol Station.

Oscar steps out of a car with the driver stepping out behind him swatting him repeatedly on the head. The driver gets back in his car, and drives off, leaving Oscar there in the Barren side of Marghcrita District. He walked to a place called 'Stone's Bar' and ordered a drink. "Dude, today was a Shitty day."

"Why's that?" Bar tender asked.

"It starts back over, like about, a hundred pages ago, or something…"

11 ● CAT PIRATE SHIP

As he'd pointed out before, Oreo 7 was headed to the Pirate Ship to learn more about *and*, stop Mr. Bigglesworth. The Pirate Ship is lined up among several space crafts by the Pussy Port along the bottom crust portion of the Taco where it 'U's. Oreo 7 was in his Space Police Suit with his bubble helmet on, using his Anti-Gravity Pack to float over from the SS Pussy Willow's Pussy Port doors to and along the Pussy Willow, headed towards the end of the C.L.I. Taurus Engine. Once he sees the Pirate ship, he floats off to the ship from underneath. Oreo 7 recognized it right away, even though it had the word 'Penetrator' painted on the side, "This is an 'Origin 58 Pounce' model. Very sleek for a Pirate Ship."

He enters into an engineering chamber that unbolts the shell lid. After taking the bolts off, he removes the lid, unscrews the hatch, and it enters a chamber. Once in the chamber, he closes the hatch behind him, re-screwing it tightly, he swims aggressively through the wires and around tubes and ducting. He then unscrews and opens the next wall layer which changes the pressure immediately! Oreo squints for a moment, and then opens the hatch.

Inside, he is able to stand, meaning the floors are gravitized from top to bottom, meaning its an expensive ship. Oreo found himself in the Cargo bay after entering the space through the engineering shaft. He put the panel he came through, back on the wall and screws it back up quickly, tightly. He'd moved among the boxes, drawing his gun, and opening his helmet to relieve his own oxygen tank.

He pointed his gun out ahead of him and listened for any sound, and he snuck silently. Moving towards the door, there's no one in site, but there's cameras everywhere, so there was no way around it, he was going to be seen. "I'm coming for myow, Mr. Bigglesworth." Oreo 7 says, and he started walking casually. He was already seen. It didn't matter.

In the next room it was more like a hangar, with a 2 person Tater Tot Ship being held by its upper hull to the ceiling, over the floor which appeared to be a massive door to drop the ship out of, a door 4 times larger than the ship itself. Across the room, across the massive door, is a large service lift. Looking back he'd also seen an Elevator in the Cargo room but it appeared to be out of service, or someone deliberately cut off its power. Oreo ran across the large door to the service lift and took it up.

Oreo could hear the laughs and camaraderie of the calicos down the halls, as the Lift had gone to the next floor up. A Calico was standing there next to the lift when it came up, and Oreo went up behind the Calico as he was turning to look behind him, putting him in a sleeper hold and knocking him out. He pulls him back on the lift with him and presses the button to go up to the next level while Oreo stayed on this one.

The second level looked like a Rockstar had trashed the Penthouse Suite. Oreo held his gun out, walking slowly along the halls; no one else was close by- but he could hear them upstairs on the ship through the loft. He appeared to be in a room that was almost just as large as the hangar below, with doors along the sides, which he'd assumed were the Calico's sleeping quarters.

Everything was thrashed, "What a waste," Oreo says, looking at such a beautiful and luxurious ship left unkept to slums, "I thought Christmas was every day." One door with a map of the SS Pussy Willow on it looked suspicious to Oreo, so he quietly walked over to it. He opens the door quickly and points the guns inside aggressively, but it's a room full cat porn! Pictures all over the wall with cats posing with shaved sexual areas wearing riskay outfits and videos in the background of cat myowking under cars and behind trash cans. Oreo 7, shuts the door.

"Down here! Someone help I'm down here!" the voice said from inside the ship.

"Shut the myowk up!" one of the Calicos yells, as Oreo looks on seriously, and uncomfortable. He sneaks quietly across the floor towards the Elevator and realizes that he can see through the glass door up and down the shaft easily, but below, the windows were sealed up. "Myow sick kittens." Oreo says, taking the safety off his gun. He looks down in the elevator shaft and sees a girl cat in there, a Savannah cat stripped down to her fur. Oreo 7 pressed the button to open the door to the elevator shaft to his level and the door opens. She's shivering.

"Are myow okay?" Oreo asks in a

whisper.

"I'm okay." She says aloud.

"I said Shut the Myowk up!" the Calicos yell down the elevator shaft at her.

Oreo pulls her out of the shaft, drags her over to a restroom, and locks the door, "Space Police. Myow're safe with me." He says to her.

"Myow're crazy, get me out of here!" she yells at him.

Oreo swats her across the face and says, "I'll get myow out of here when I'm good and ready. Now… go over there and take a shit while I finish what I came here to do. Myow'll be alright, now where is he?"

"How the myowk am I supposed to know?" she yells at him.

"Keep myow voice down," Oreo says calmly, "myow sound like a boat full of trash."

"Just get me off this ship!" she yells at him.

He Swats her across the face again, "I'll put myow back in there bitch, don't push me."

There's a pause and a silence a moment. Oreo reiterates with some personal affection, rare among felines, "Listen, I came here to destroy this organization, and that's what I'm going to do, so I need myow to go sit on the shit box and wait until I get back, do myow understand me?"

"No! Don't myow leave me here myow myowkin' male chauvinist! No! He's crazy! He'll kill everyone!"

Oreo 7 Swats her across the face 4 times because 3 times wasn't enough. "Are myow finished?" Oreo was. He turns around and goes out the door, closing her in and locking the door from outside with a contraption he places over the latch that solidifies after he put it there. Only he can open the door now. "Dumb bitch." He mumbles.

He took the lift up to the next floor with the Calico still out cold on it and upon arriving to that level, he sees the entire Calico gang sitting and standing around a dining room table gambling high on Catnip. It was as if the curtains opened up on Oreo 7 standing alone with a Calico body in the corner of a vast elevator lift. The entire table looks over and sees him, and the negative vibrations buzzed. Oreo 7 points his gun up at them and open fires at them as they immediately spaz! The table flies up in the air with money, chips, cards, drinks, everything, spilling everywhere and the cats dart off in chaos!

They all head up the steps at the other end of the ship to the top floor inside the Pirate Ship. Oreo knew he couldn't pull this off alone, but the least he could do was capture Mr. Bigglesworth and find out where Maximus Cataclysma is. He runs after the Calicos up the steps to the top floor where the main bridge to the ship is and a loft overlooking the floor below. Oreo starts firing his gun off at all of them as they immediately jump over the edge of the paw rail and run away to grab weapons quickly!

At the end of the loft walk, there's the Captain's Quarters, and Oreo ran straight to the door. He puts his back to the door with his gun lifted, ready to point and fire-pushes back and the door opens with him pointing everywhere in the room! It's absolutely thrashed inside. There's water tanks sitting on top of tables in the room with Cat parts in them like legs, arms, heads, sick twisted things. The room 'S'ed around so Oreo was careful around each turn looking to find Mr. Bigglesworth. The S of the room only had more doors which seemed to lead to more... laboratories whereas Oreo 7 originally thought this was a

Captain's quarters and maybe it was before, but now it was the most customized piece of the ship, and the worst customization job ever done. The architecture is so dreadful it's straight out of a horror film.

Suddenly the lights go out in the entire ship…

From outside the ship on the SS Pussy Willow, all the ships are lit up, and then that specific one goes completely black among the stars and the darkness of space.

Oreo's eyes adjust, but the dark is so much so, that he can barely see anything at all. Instead of trying, he put a pair of X-ray goggles on to see beyond light reflection in opacity.

Oreo 7 crept silently and slowly as if nearly nonexistent, back out of the room and along the walk of the loft, staying down to hide his heat signature. But then he thought about it a moment and sighed. He was done with this shit, Oreo had enough. He pulled out a tiny explosive and tossed it over the loft side and it explodes with meow-screams as guns shot fire off everywhere! Oreo runs down the steps as they curve down to point back towards the butt-end of the ship. The Calicos are firing everywhere aimless in the dark, while Oreo waits behind the corner watching in his goggles.

There he is! Oreo 7 sees Mr. Bigglesworth on the 3rd floor below at the bottom of the loft point and he jumps over the paw-rail down to the 3rd floor and lands right on top of Mr. Bigglesworth as they roll. Mr. Bigglesworth grabs a long broom stick from the corner of the room that never had a purpose up until now, and he starts whacking the back of Oreo 7 with it! Oreo drops his gun as it slides all the way across the floor to the other side of the room!

Mr. Bigglesworth takes the broomstick to a glass container with Emergency gear inside, shattering the glass, and setting off an Emergency Alert system in the ship! The lights strobe black, red and white! Oreo gets up and Swats Mr. Bigglesworth across the face! Suddenly there's an Explosion from the upper deck!

"What is that from?" Oreo 7 Asks.

Mr. Bigglesworth grabs an Axe out of the Emergency container and swings it at Oreo, trimming his whisker! Now they're offset! Another Explosion goes off and the stars outside the ship start shifting, as it appears they're steadily heading towards the SS Pussy Willow! "Myow piece of shit. This is all myow fault!"

Oreo Swats him across the face 2 times, "It's always my fault, mother myowker." He takes the Emergency Container door, rips it off, and smacks Mr. Bigglesworth across the face- his shades fly off- his hat spinning in the air. Another Explosion, Oreo Swats Mr. Bigglesworth in the face again, only this time he swats him good and puts Mr. B's lights out. Oreo walks back to that bathroom door and pulls the contraption off, and grabs the Savannah cat girl by the arm, "C'mon bitch, hurry up."

He pushes Mr. Bigglesworth onto the lift, and it takes them down to the bottom level where the '2 cat' Tater Tot Ship is being held up on the ceiling. Oreo goes to a panel on the wall and has the ship lowered, as blasts are happening on the upper deck. The Ship lowers it's ramp and Oreo drags Mr. Bigglesworth onto the ship, putting him in the 2nd cat seat, strapping him in. He grabs large and thick plastic cargo bags and tells her, "Myow can trust me, get in the bag."

"Myow're just gonna throw me in some bag?" She asks.

"Listen," Oreo says sternly as explosions are going off in the background, "Myow're just some hoe I found on this ship! But if myow get in the bag, I'll save myow life, now, shut up n' get in there!" As explosion are going off everywhere, she gets in irritably. He takes masking tape and seals the bag air tight, then masks the bag in the tape, then makes a rope out of the rest of the roll of the tape, and ties it to the back of the Tater Tot ship. Oreo 7 gets in the ship, gets behind the controls, turns it on, opens the massive garage door, and ejects the Tater Tot with the Savannah cat in a plastic bag on a tape rope out of the Pirate Ship, just seconds before it explodes for no reason at all.

Oscar drives the Tater Tot ship through the Pussy Port into the Puss City, landing the Tater Tot outside the B Side Pussy Patrol Station near the Deluxe Supreme Mall. The Pussy Willow Media arrives with Cameras and Reporters quickly, as the door opens and Oreo drags Mr. Bigglesworth out of the ship and gives him over to the Pussy Patrol cops that are walking upon the situation.

Suddenly Ms. Twinkle Toes walks up to Oreo 7 and says, "What happened? How did myow get ahold of Mr. Bigglesworth?"

"I think what matters is that I got ahold of Mr. Bigglesworth." Oreo 7 says. He walks over to the plastic bag as it's moving around rapidly and Princess the Savannah cat is meow-screaming inside. The news cameras are all watching as Oreo cuts the bag open and the cat bolts out of the bag so quick they could only catch a smear of her.

There's a giant 'BANG' heard outside the entire SS Pussy Willow as the Pirate Ship finally hit the shell of the Taco Space City and exploded, putting a burn mark on the Taco.

12 • INTERROGATORS

Shallow waits worried in the Pussy Patrol Station in Deluxe Supreme. She's alone pacing the floor inside the lobby, when she sees him walking in, buzzing hard on a few drinks and walking through the front doors of the Station. She stood there looking like a poor kitten, helpless and wanting. He walks up to her and says her name, "Shallow."

"I couldn't think about anything else." She says.

"Uh... I mean, yeah... yeah, me neither baby." He says. "I'm sorry, I've been preoccupied."

"After everything that's happened, it should be me who should be sorry." she says.

He thinks a moment, "Well that's actually kind of true, myow know?"

"What do myow mean?" she asks.

"Well," he says, "I'm constantly heading towards a dangerous situation, and myow're too beautiful to be in the middle of that. I don't know what I'd do if I lost myow, except start seeing other cats. But if myow still feel the same way about me now, I can tell myow, my feelings are still the same for myow. But if myow don't feel the same... I have a confession."

"A confession?" she follows.

"Yes."

"What is it?"

"Myow make me wanna hold myow down in some tall grass and pound it like a SWAT team breaking down a do."

"Oh!" she says overwhelmed by his comment.

"Yeah," he says, "Rough, invasive, and lots of vocalization... like it's supposed to be."

"Well then..." she says... getting closer to him and holding his paws, "Myow paws are cold... and there's alcohol on myow breath."

He reassures her, "Those are all signs of dominant stamina."

"Oh!" she says overwhelmed again.

Shadow who is paw cuffed to the table, sits in the interrogation room as Muffins and Oscar who walk in quietly. They were roughed up like Shadow looked, only they look angry and serious yet calm.

Shadow looked amused. They sit down at the table in front of Shadow who doesn't hesitate to ask, "Tell me Muffins… Oscar… if I were sitting on the other side of this table, would myow show me mercy?" they stare at him… and he continues, "so, myow're Muffins and Oscar…"

"And myow're Cataclysma's bell cat." Oscar says.

"I'm an Assassin, no one owns me. It's a dirty career but the clients keep coming. There is always another cat waiting to die… because cats can spare 8."

"well myow have to admit, it's gotta ring to it. 'Cataclysma's Bell Cat'."

"Are myow the Nick-name manager?" Shadow asks, "the 'Stupid Ones'?"

"Stupid ones?"

"Nick names. They're out there." Shadows says, "I'm actually surprised that myow caught me."

Muffins says calmly, "While myow were a kitten still licking myow butt hole, I was trained to lick lives off cats like a popsicle."

"Intimidating." Shadow brushes it off sarcastically.

"Where's Cataclysma?" Muffins

asks. "Where the myowk is Cataclysma myow dumb cat?"

Shadow reiterates, "Let's just say he's having… a really good time."

"I can sit in here and mind-myowk myow all day, Shadow." Oscar stands up speaking, "I can mind-myowk myow real good."

"Myow think myow're in control," Shadow says, "But at any moment I could turn the tables somehow, break free, kidnap Shallow… maybe tonight I'll make her open up a can of fish and I'll sniff her butt."

"Myow sack of cucumbers," Oscar says, "If myow weren't Cataclysma's Bell Cat, would myow be any different?"

"Cataclysma is a client," Shadow says, "he got what he paid for."

"What difference does that make?" Muffins asks.

"Because I've never been to his mansion, I've never even seen it!" Shadow exclaims, "Myow could sit here and mind-myowk me all myow want, still won't change the fact that myow're looking for crunchy food… in a soft food can."

"Myow're a liar." Muffins says.

"I guess there is no mutual respect here then, is there?" Shadow asks.

"Respect is not attracted to myow."
Muffins says, "Respect runs from myow…
it's afraid of myow. Respect thinks myow
looks like a monster that was chewed on and
spit out and survived to look like it."

"As of right now," Shadow says, "I
guarantee myow, where ever Cataclysma is,
he's laughing, right now."

"Where is Cataclysma?"

"I don't know, but IF… I could call a
guy." Shadow says, "All I would have to do
is make one phone call, and in a matter time,
this entire police station will be destroyed."

"That's a big if." Muffins says.

"There is no way myow come out of
this with any sort of victory." Oscar says.

"I don't doubt it, I don't doubt
everything myow say is true, but myow will
never catch Cataclysma. However, there is
something I *CAN* tell myow: If myow can
squeeze everything myow have got around
Mr. Bigglesworth, myow will catch
Cataclysma without a problem *and it won't
be because of me*. That's the important part,
because that means my record as an
Assassin is clean and myow can catch
Cataclysma. So, why don't we discuss that
instead? Because like I said, I've never been
to his mansion… but the Nip-Runners

have."

Muffins and Oscar look on at Shadow with consideration, and there's a pause a moment to think it through. Oscar finally says, "I'm listening."

Oreo 7 and Mr. Bigglesworth are inside the interrogation room sitting at the table, it's a typical scene. Mr. Bigglesworth doesn't look his best, he looks very roughed up, and Oreo has removed his jacket so that he's there in his dress shirt and vest. Mr. Bigglesworth is purring at the table, looking away antagonizing Oreo if he can.

"Does it affect myow?" Mr. Bigglesworth asks Oreo 7, "To know just how Sociopathic myow truly are? Does it make myow feel anything at all that myow brought that ratchet cat back to the Pussy Willow in a Plastic bag?"

"Where is Cataclysma?" Oreo 7 asks bluntly.

"It depends." Mr. Bigglesworth says.

"What difference does it make?" Oreo asks.

"Depends on whether or not he releases another special surprise on the SS Pussy Willow. If he does, he is at his

Mansion. If he doesn't, it's because he decided to forget about the whole thing and went to party it up in the SS Phadazz on the other side of the Gas Giant."

"The big one."

"Yes," Mr. Bigglesworth says, "He likes to flash."

"If this is just some bird corpse on a rubber band hanging from the ceiling to myow..." Oreo gets up, "I'm gonna need a warm bowl of milk."

"Look at that," Mr. Bigglesworth says, "he's already tapping out."

"Not exactly." Oreo 7 says as Muffins and Oscar walk into the Interrogation room.

"So this is the abstract painting that unleashed the myowking Tapeworms on the myowking Space Police Station." Muffins exclaims, "How appropriate."

"Hey, that wasn't me!" Mr. Bigglesworth exclaims, "I just move Catnip!"

"Myow want to destroy the law," Oscar says getting in Bigglesworth's face, "Yet there was no one to protect myow from 'chance'!"

Mr. Bigglesworth shrugs putting his paws up with innocence, "I don't know anything, I just work for criminals. Maybe it was a social science experiment… and it went really well. Myow took in Pudder, then the Tapeworm splashed out of his butt hole into the Police Station and now the entire station is completely shut down. Myow'll have to scorch the entire hull and rebuild just to get rid of that infestation. Sounds to me like Max outsmarted myow good."

"Where's Cataclysma?" Muffins asks.

Bigglesworth says, "The Space Police want myow Special Cops gone so they can go back to the way things were, when they had it controlled. But I know the truth, there's no going back, I'm nick-naming it 'the Cataclysma'."

"Why are myow trying to kill Space Police Officers?" Muffins asks.

"I'm not trying to kill Cops!" Biggleworth says, "I just work for a guy that wants to kill Cops. Don't shoot the messenger."

"Do myow even have any rational fear," Oscar asks, "or are myow off the deep end?"

"I'm a functioning member of cat-ciety!" He yells.

Oscar antagonizes, "If myow fart in

the hot tub and there's no bubbles, myow know myow're in trouble, right?"

"What do myow mean?" Mr. Bigglesworth asks perplexed by the question, "I know when a fart is a fart- I can tell the difference!"

Oscar says, "Myow're a vile glue slime on the back of a slug. Myow're fish bones stealing meat from a chicken."

"Don't talk to me like myow're a saint because myow're not! Myow're cats! To the Space Police Force, myow're just the next recruit- the expendable front line dying to protect the psychopathic wealthy fat cats of places like Double Cheese and the Whopper Ring. I'm no monster guys, other than the fact that I keep the hoes locked up in my elevator."

Muffins Swats Mr. Bigglesworth and says, "That's for all the hoes myow kept in myow elevator."

"Where is Cataclysma?!" Oscar yells at him.

"I don't know! He's not my child!" Mr. Bigglesworth yells, "I just work for him!"

"I have one child," Muffins says as he raises his paw at Mr. Bigglesworth's face, "And I call him 'The Sensation'."

"If I tell myow where Cataclysma is, myow have to give me what I want." Mr. Bigglesworth says.

"What do myow want?" Oscar asks.

"My Lawyers down at the front desk have already written up my terms." Mr. Bigglesworth say, "So even if I ask for something, and tell myow where he is, myow can't ditch out on delivering. He's always at his mansion."

"What Mansion?"

"Myow know that one in Santa Meownica… when myow're headed straight to the beach down Main and, myow know that point past central where it forks?"

"Yeah?"

"And there's always that homeless cat on the corner with the myowkin' three string acoustic guitar singing songs about how he's 'dyin'-in-the-street' all the time?"

"Yeah yeah…"

"Okay well just past that point there's another street…"

"Right…"

"Yeah and that street has streets that are also next to it."

Muffins grabs Mr. Bigglesworth's head and pushes it down to the interrogation table, "Where is the myowking mansion myow son of a bitch?!"

Mr. Bigglesworth yells "In Santa Meownica!"

Oscar pulls out a gun and puts it to Mr. Bigglesworth's head as Mr. B meow-screams, Oscar yells, "Can't deliver demands to a DEAD Cat!"

"If myow kill me, myow'll die too!"

"Fine!" Oscar says putting his gun back in his is holster and grabbing a hammer from another pocket, "I'm more of a knee-cap kind of cat anyway."

Outside the interrogation room, they meet with Shallow, Oreo 7 and Ms. Twinkle Toes. Muffins says, "I know where Cataclysma is. He's at his Mansion on Cat Planet in Santa Meownica, on 420 Catpiss Rd."

"Ok." Ms. Twinkle Toes says as they immediately jump to their feet and leave! "We've been active non-stop, I think everyone needs to rest. Prepare myow breakfasts. Spend time with myow loved ones, for tonight… we dine in a box of lit fire crackers."

The next morning, In the dressing room, Muffins, Oscar, Oreo 7, and Shallow are suiting up for the raid. Oscar opens his locker and shows everyone an outfit that he has, "Everyone come here. Look at this." He says. The outfit is unevenly vertically striped in different shades of green, he says, "So, because the Criminal is not complex with like… a lot of details, I realized what I truly fear is actually something inside myself. Maybe I fear my own ability cuz like… I get mad sometimes and like I could do some terrible shit. So, I got all spiritual and took a journey inwards with a lit candle and some good smells because… I was ready. Because like, in order to defeat fear, myow have to like… **BE** it. Like.. myow know? Like yeah… like… myow gotta like… *bask* in the fear of other cats and like… I DID. And that's when I decided I wanted to defeat crime with the most terrifying costume… and become something even more terrifying than a normal scary thing. So I thought I should became a scary idea, right? So I did what most cast won't do."

"What's that?" Shallow asks.

"I went for a trip out in the country, and walked through the Cucumber fields back on Cat Planet." The others seemed uneasy at hearing this, "I could feel the fear overwhelming me and like, distorting my reality n' shit, trying to control me. And I was like, 'No way!' but like... yeah. So, I knew the power to scare cats could be mine if I embraced my worst fear. So, there I was, screaming out of my myowkin' mind in the middle of a cucumber field... becoming one with the terror, trying to focus, concentrate and use my abilities while in the fields of cucumbers. That's when I knew what I must become..." He turns and looks at them with the suit visible behind him, "I must become... 'Cucumber Cat'."

"That's myowking stupid." Muffins says, "Don't put the suit on."

Suddenly Twinkle Toes walks in and says, "We can't leave yet."

"Why?" Shallow asks.

"It's Bonkers."

13 ● GONE BONKERS

The SS Pussy Willow begins to rotate in a way that is unnatural to the city, causing public alarm! The light and the shadows along the city inside were shifting in an almost quick and steady manner. There's uneasy meowing all around the city. The Extra Pussies walk out of the Pussy Patrol Station; Muffins the Grey Maine Coon, Shallow the British Blue, Oreo 7 the Manx in a Tux, and Oscar the Orange Tabby dressed as a Cucumber. They witness everything happening. They're all suited up in their Space Police Uniforms except for Oscar, dressed as a Cucumber. When cats walk by, if they weren't already uneasy about the ship rotating a little quicker than usual, they look over and see Oscar in his Cucumber outfit and all they see is a Cucumber... and they just hiss and run away. Muffins sees this and says, "Okay, maybe it's kind of cool."

Dr. Bonkers had a gun to Captain Peyimess', forcing her to leave the Control Bridge of the SS Pussy Willow, "I can't wait to show myow my new toy!" he says to her! Dr. Bonkers takes Captain Peyimess in a cat taxi to the middle of Double Cheese and put the Captain in a chair in the middle of an alley. It was hard for the Captain to see anything. Everything was draped with large long cloth strips like massive ribbons. This Selkirk cat had devised some sort of evil contraption!

Suddenly a Pussy Patrol Officer spots Dr. Bonkers in the alley from the end and radios it in, "I have suspect in site. Location Double Cheese. I repeat, Dr. Bonkers is in Double Cheese, Burn Alley."

"It would probably feel good to be weightless one last time, wouldn't it?" Dr. Bonkers asks. Terrified Captain Peyimess, confused by his comment, is lost for a single word. He pulls a lever, and the Chair rises up immediately- a sling shot chair with bungee cords as high as the tallest one way gravitized building. Bonkers slings the poor cat across the 0-Gravity Divide of the Taco, towards the other side of the Taco, watching the poor cat meow-scream as she shrinks to a red little splat in the distance, hitting the 'A Side' surface street. Dr. Bonkers laughs hysterically, "I love science!"

Oreo 7 says to Muffins and Oscar, "Myow two handle the Control Bridge, Shallow and I will handle Dr. Bonkers."

"NO!" She says, "I don't ever want to see that cat again!"

"We'll handle the myowking curly haired dust bunny," Muffins says, "Myow take care of the Bridge."

"But I want Oscar to help me with the bridge!" Shallow says.

"Oscar stays with me," Muffins says, "his costume will psychologically control Dr. Bonkers. I need his Cucumber *INSIDE* this Pussy."

There's a pause as they all see eye to eye.

"I completely understand," Oreo 7 says, "Shallow and I will take care of the Control Bridge."

Dr. Bonkers has the Pussy Patrol Officer in the chair now as the Officer is hissing and squirming erratically, meow-threatening Dr. Bonkers. "Myow're going to Hell in a Cat Travel Cage!" Muffins suddenly disrupt Dr. Bonkers with his aura and presence; Bonkers turns around and sees

Muffins, "Well well…" Bonkers says, "so pleasantly surprised to see myow." Bonkers walks closer towards Muffins. Behind him, Oscar comes walking around the chair; the officer seeing the cucumber and meow-screaming more!

"Do myow think myow'll go to Heaven when myow die, Dr. Bonkers? Do myow think myow'll go to Heaven after myow just killed 1 of 3 Captains on this ship?!" Muffins asks.

"If Heaven is a place, where I own a massive house and several massive human servants who feed me and massage my neck and back on a daily basis while I lay around and piss on everything, then yeah, I've already been there… and the food sucks, Muffins. *I CAME BACK*… because I like a good *meal*."

"But nobody loves myow." Muffins says.

"Small price to pay to have it my way." Dr. Bonker says. "when I wear somebody's face and look in the Mirror on a full belly, it's like I see my reflection, only I don't."

"If myow do not surrender now," Muffins says, "Myow will face the death penalty after we catch myow."

"What makes myow so certain myow'll catch me?" Dr. Bonkers asks.

"The Cucumber behind myow." Muffins says. Dr. Bonkers turns around and the moment seemed to freeze in time as pure terror struck him, the entire moment happening like slow motion. All he could see was a cucumber, he didn't see Oscar at all, he just saw this… big long… green… inseminating shaped… cucumber… looking right at him. The Officer in the chair hysterically writhing in terror and screaming insanely didn't help Bonkers feel any better, as the frequencies penetrated his head! He just stood there in the meow-screams of sincere horror! The Cucumber began to psychologically infect Dr. Bonkers! All he could see was terror and fear, loathing the cucumber; eager to escape from the cucumber! The Cucumber psychedelically mind melted his thought feeling colors! Muffins Grabs Dr. Bonkers and says, "I think we've made an agreement." Putting him in paw cuffs.

14 ● THE MANSION

Oscar, Muffins, Shallow, Oreo 7, Ms. Twinkle Toes, and Dr. Bonkers is strapped into the dolly and face guard again; The Extra Pussies get on a Space Police S.W.A.T. Ship, and exit the SS Pussy Willow Intergalactic Taco Space City through the Pussy Port, and travel to the 'Jump Gate', where they travel through a Worm hole back to Cat Planet.

Once in orbit, the Extra Pussies board a Space Police Lasagna Shuttle, taking it down to Santa Meownica off the Clawifornia coast. Once there, the Lasagna shuttle hovers over the area before raiding the location. Looking up from the ground, the cats could see the shuttle in the sky, as one big slice of Lasagna, floating there for no apparent reason.

As Oscar is getting ready, Shallow walks up to him and says, "Myow don't have to leave."

"I do," he says, "It's my job."

She looks down and says, "I'm afraid."

"Hey," he says, "don't be." He turns

around to be mellow dramatic and soft.

Shallow says, "Wait…"

"What?"

She kisses him and it's a longer kiss than last time, and after a moment of sappy kissing and the reader holding in vomit, they finally stop… and she says, "Is that a better kiss?"

"No. Not really." He says. She looks disappointed, and he caves, "Shallow, I'm sorry."

"Don't be." She says, "Love means when myow says sorry, it comes with sensual favors."

"Yeah I know." He says.

"Do myow really care about me?" she asks.

"Well I mean like… yeah baby, yeah." he says, juggling other rationalizations in his mind. "Myow are like, the reason why cats spray everything."

"If I find out myow're myowkin' other cats, I'll myowkin' kill myow." She says.

"I'll keep that variable in mind while we're together." He says.

"Do myow swear?" she asks.

"Baby, I myowkin' swear all the time."

"Okay." She says and they hug as he looks away rolling his eyes. Shallow continues, "A racoon can love a penguin, but how will they agree on real estate?"

"We're both cats." He says.

There's a pause and she says suddenly calmly enthused… "…Oh yeah."

At deploy deck of the Lasagna Shuttle, the team stands ready to go. "He said the address is 420 Catpiss Road." Oscar says.

"He's lying." Dr. Bonkers says, "As usual. I don't put it past Mr. Bigglesworth to lie."

"Then where is the Mansion?" Muffins asks.

"I don't know" Dr. Bonkers says.

"Then how would myow know if he's lying?" Shallow asks.

"I know it's the right house." Oreo 7 says, "don't ask me how I know, just trust me."

"I don't trust anyone." Muffins says, obviously lying, "I am totally jaded because someone hurt my feelings. So, I'm going in alone. Don't argue with me about it or I'll start crying. If I need myow, if the situation becomes too much for me, I'll call myow in. Otherwise I'll tell myow I've confirmed it when I radio myow , then myow'll know… I've determined that Maximus Cataclysma is in the Mansion."

"Agreed." Ms. Twinkle Toes says.

"Bullshit." Dr. Bonkers sees right through it, and says, "Myow just want to play with myow food, before myow eat it."

Muffins readies to leave as he says, "There's nothing better than killing myow enemies, to see them run from myow, even though they're too slow, and then myow tap their girlfriend afterwards."

Dr. Bonkers says, "I can respect that."

Muffins drops onto a raft in the ocean with black war paint striped across his body, dressed in all green like a Contra Ambush and drives it forward to the sandy beach edge. He Drags the boat up the shore to a bush, grabbing a duffle bag and a machine gun from the raft. Muffins runs up behind a militarized Racoonian guard at a mission post just off the beach side, snapping his racoon neck and killing him instantly. A little ways out in from the post is the mansion's back yard that Muffins could see through the trees. Muffins rigs explosives along the walls of the Mission. The guard suddenly notices him, but he quickly SWATs his face and knocks him out.

Muffins runs out from behind the mission carrying his duffle bag and machine gun, when a tower guard sees him and starts firing a machine gun at him! Muffins turns around and returns fire with his machine gun, tattering bullets all over the Racoonian guard as he falls from the towers! The Alarm sounds! Two more militarized Racoonians run out of the mission, and Muffin's guns them down like wet dogs getting hit by a diesel truck! More racoon soldiers begin to exit with their guns drawn, firing off, and Muffins turns around and machine guns them while bullets rapidly pop the beach sand around him! Muffins pulls out a remote and presses the button, and the entire mission explodes into a massive fireball billowing out into a black cloud! Racoons rained from the sky in their own blood all over Muffins as he says, "I think myow came down with something."

In the distance, Cobalt could hear the explosion as he was wearing all black, sneaking into the house. He knew right away, "It's the Space Police." He says. He goes back to breaking in through the window discretely, no one notices him... Cobalt wanders up the hall of the Mansion to the master bedroom on the 2nd floor, pacing himself to have the energy to face Cataclysma himself. Cobalt pulls his gun out with the silencer tip, pointed diagonal up as he jumped his whole body into the door, busting it open! He swings his gun pointed around the room, but Max isn't in there and the window is open with the drapes blowing in and out like a mess. Cobalt runs to the window! He goes to look out it and sees Cataclysma the pale hairless sphynx cat in black pants, black fur coat, and lots of sparkling jewelry, already at the other end of the court within the Mansion's architecture. Max laughed, "Ehehehehe!" He was heading for the Garage, and Cobalt knew it. He jumped out the window and ran after Cataclysma.

At the Front entrance, while the Racoonian soldiers are investigating the explosion at the back along the beach, there are guards with jeeps who have closed off the Mansion. The entrance is completely surrounded. Muffins steps out from behind the side corner of the property and start pulling the trigger on his machine gun, unloading lead like 'back-to-school' stationary stores, popping off one racoon after another! The bullets spatter across a racoon looking like a mouse with red painted feet ran across his chest and face! They drop to the ground and the energy is high level!

After the soldiers are down, Muffins runs over to the front entrance door, about 50 yards away, pulling a bazooka out of the duffle bag. Behind him, a jeep full of terrorist cats with machine guns, race out from behind the corner side of the property. Muffins hears them, spins around quickly and fires! The missile hits the engine, and the car pops and explodes with the terrorist cats flying out everywhere meow-screaming!

Muffins turns back around and blows a hole in the front door to get into the Mansion property. More guns begin firing off behind him as he runs in through the burning gates and away from the road, out into the foliage of the trees and bushes that surround the mansion along it's perimeter walls. They run hard behind him like panthers in the jungle, and Muffins stops instantly, turns around and SWATs one of them down in mid-air, and machine guns the other one behind him down with his left paw- they jiggle like bacon on a fork before hitting the ground! Muffins takes quickly to a position behind another bush on the far-left corner facing the Mansion.

From the trees is a fresh cut lawn that reaches out for 100 paws before the sidewalk to the Mansion side. The entire property is suddenly crawling with militarized racoons, all of them coming out of the mansion with machine guns! Muffins points out towards a new cat face and kills each one of them individually one by one as he pulls the trigger and bullets spray out! The soldiers shoot back but for some reason, it's like trying to catch a red laser light on the wall!

The Soldiers running across the lawn at him do a seizure shake as the bullets run across their fuzzy bodies! A Racoonian tries to come at Muffins from his right but Muffins is sharp as a Razor- he turns around and loads the racoon full of bullets like a jackpot at a Casino! "You're a Lucky

Winner." Muffins spits on the racoons body as more of the soldiers keep coming across the lawn at him from the Mansion so Muffins pulls a Grenade out of the duffle bag and tosses it over to the lawn and BOOM! Racoons fly everywhere screaming while Muffins is mowing down the rest of them still running towards him!

Muffins runs over to a huge statue to take cover while the bullets are popping edges off the concrete! He turns around, from beside the Statue, and pops a good one right in the nearest racoon and says, "Take a hit, bro."

Muffins throws another grenade out and takes out a entire flowerbed, with racoons flying out from the bang! Muffins runs over to another statue base, taking cover carefully. Muffins looked up and could see his main problem was the machine gunner on the balcony.

Muffins decided quickly that he needed to strategize, taking out the other racoon on the balcony. While running, Muffins fires off his machine gun at the racoons and takes cover behind a ledge wall in the garden, no higher than a foot. Muffins tosses another grenade at them and racoon guts spatter across the green grass. Muffins gets up and starts firing off bullets one by one on each racoon with precision! His machine gun dead, he pulls out a paw-gun and fires at one more racoon, popping a hole in his head! Pow! pow! He shoots another one! The Soldiers tighten up and hold their ground carefully. Muffins sees another soldier racoon hiding behind a bush and says, "This is what happens when I catch myow racoons, roughing up a pussy's bush." He pulls the trigger and pops a bullet in that racoon! Got him!

Muffins pulls out a shotgun! The racoon on the balcony still firing off the machine gun at him, Muffins fires rapidly with the cocking of the shot gun, blasting the face off one racoon and blowing another racoon right in half! Muffins runs through the walkway with the pink flowers next to them! As he ran firing the gun off, the pink flowers were getting blasted by all the gun fire following behind as he ran; bushes and chips of statues and ledges flying up and all over!

One of the racoons throws a grenade at Muffins as it hits him square in the face and lands on the ground next to him! He jumps into the air wildly squirming and angry-meowing frantically as it explodes making Muffins fly higher and over into a dense bush next to a gardening shed! He limps over to the shed quickly and closes himself inside while the guns fired off outside.

Inside the shed, Muffins scoped out all the sharp objects, a Hoe, a Rake, Pitch Forks, Machetes, Saw blades. He takes off his gear and reaches into a wound on his side and pulls a bullet out and throws it on the floor. "Myowk myow." He says.

The Racoonian Soldiers surround the gardening shed outside, machine guns in paw. Muffins hears them even though they're trying to be quiet, and he jumps up at the ceiling. "Fire!" the racoon yells, and the soldiers all fire their machine guns at the shed, shredding the walls with bullet holes; the Windows blown out, the door chopped in holes, the walls chaotically polka dotted! Then they stopped shooting... and looked at each other. One of them walks over slowly to check the door- he opens it slowly until it's wide open... and walks in. From the ceiling, a Hoe swings down and chops the racoon's neck with blood squirting out like a water fountain! Muffins kicks the racoon over! He throws the pitchfork at one of them with his right paw and nails the son-of-a-bitch in the chest! He turns to his other side and throws the saw blades at another racoon and they tag the racoon's face, neck, and cutting off the racoon's leg! Muffins grabs an axe and chops another soldier's legs off with a swift swing and dropping the axe! Muffins runs over and grabs one of their machine guns and starts unloading it on the next wave of oncoming soldiers!

Muffins runs and ducks, taking cover behind a bush of white flowers rowed up the walk path! The racoons all fire at his general area, and Muffins stands up and fires back left to right with non-stop bullets sowing into the racoon soldier crowd! He chopped the flowers level as he walked up the path firing the machine gun at them, the entire yard loading up with racoon bodies. He finally turns around and starts firing at that racoon on the balcony as bullets blow holes in his face, chest and arm! He falls over the paw-rail and brakes his neck hitting the ground! Muffins says, "Looks like he fell asleep on the job."

Muffins ran up on some epic roman steps with statue-esc ledges and corners, and the racoon soldiers start running down the steps from the top as Muffins stops and pulls the trigger! The entire scape is sprayed with bullets as Muffins can't even hold the gun still anymore so, he just waves it around and hopes it kills everything! After firing he looks out to see if he missed anything... and then keeps moving!

Muffins runs up on the massive back porch fixture, about 100 paws of concrete tiles in precision with fountains and statues about them. Two Soldiers on alert before the stairs see Muffins roll up, but Muffins pulls the trigger, chucking the one racoon up, but the other got his head chopped off by the blast of the machine gun bullets and falls into the water fountain. Muffins climbed up through the cement landscaping and up the side of the house, getting up on the roof of the Mansion, running across the top and down onto a balcony side where he could get in through a window.

After breaking in the room and out the door, Muffins began walking up the halls, saying, "Here Cataclysma. Pspspspsps. I gotta surprise for myow." One of the racoon soldiers inside the house sees Muffins and fires the gun, but Muffins is quicker on the draw and puts him down, taking his machine gun.

Up the hall, Lucky was walking

toward Muffins with his gun ready. At the elbow of the hallway, Muffins turns the corner and they both meet eyes! Muffins runs back to take cover behind the corner of the wall as Lucky fires the machine gun at Muffins, destroying the wall! Muffins swings his machine gun around the corner and fires at Lucky as he leaps at a door breaking it down and into the room! Muffins runs over to a statue and kneels behind it as he fires back at Lucky, the walls and glass around him bursting with holes! Lucky runs away back down the hall and Muffins runs after him! As soon as Muffins gets around the next corner Lucky is waiting there and pulls the trigger, machine gunning the hallway as Muffin jumps for cover behind the corner!

Lucky runs up the steps of the mansion quickly to get higher ground. Muffins hears him and goes running behind him! Lucky turns around and fires off to keep Muffins from coming around the corner! Lucky yells, "I'm a puppet in this, Muffins! I want legal immunity!"

Muffins runs out from behind the corner and slides across the floor as he fires the machine gun at Lucky, bullet holes impaling Lucky head to toe! He hits the floor in a red puddle and lets out a last breath! Muffins says, "Myow immune system shut down."

For a moment, the Mansion is silent from all the violence, but Muffins could still hear the racoon soldiers running around out there. Muffins grabs an orange out of a bowl on a small stand table by the steps, and tosses it into Lucky's puddle of blood and says, "Here Lucky, have a blood Orange."

Muffins pulls up his radio and says, "Muffins to Twinkle Toes, Its confirmed. Over."

15 ● CATACLYSMA

Cobalt follows Cataclysma, and sees him go through a door in the garage. When Cobalt walks up to that door and opens it, it's a closet for cleaning utilities. He pulls on some kind of lever on the wall and the wall inside flips on a vertical pole, so that a cat can walk past it; a rotating door. Cobalt leaves the door open, and the secret door as well... walking in to follow Cataclysma.

At the front, Space Police have the driveway swarmed with cops, and the militarized cats are still shooting back defiantly. Oscar, Oreo 7, and Shallow secure the front of the house and move in with their guns drawn *except for Dr. Bonkers*, ready to fire on any racoon ready to myowk with them. Inside the Mansion, there's racoon soldiers posted up, blocking the police from the stairwell at the center of the house. Oscar and Oreo 7 open fire at them and they take cover. Oscar and Oreo 7 runs up the steps while Shallow shoots at the racoons with guns! They scatter to get away! Oreo 7 Shoots up and ahead at the racoons upstairs as they take cover! Oscar runs up ahead of them and pulls the trigger!

Shallow, Oscar, and Oreo 7 rush down the hall looking for the Master bedroom, with Dr. Bonkers following slowly behind, and find the door busted open. they run in and see the window open and the drapes blowing in the air. Shallow runs to the window and looks out as it sees across the courtyard located in the very middle of the entire house. Just past the courtyard was another large portion of the house connected to a big garage. Shallow says, "There's a Panic Room."

They jump out the window and run across the courtyard to the garage's back door, running in and seeing the open door to the closet of cleaning utilities. Oreo 7, Shallow, Dr. Bonker and Oscar head in through the door down the hall to the end opening another door into a room only to see themselves in another garage; Muffins has his gun pointed at Cobalt, and Cobalt has his pointed at Muffins, with Cataclysma standing next to a row of hummer like vehicles for cats, facing the open garage door way going out and up the hill side.

"I've come here to eat fish and

myowk myow up." Muffins says, "and I'm still looking for the fish."

"In thirty seconds myow'll be dead," Cobalt says, "and I'll explode this place and be home in time to myowk some cat under a car."

Then Muffins hears them come in without looking back and says, "Stop, he's mine."

"Myow have nothing." Cobalt says, "He's *MINE*, and myow're just the final ribbon."

"He's myow employer," Muffins says, "Why?"

"Because I have Tapeworms!" Cobalt says, "At any moment... I could splash. And if it's going to happen, it's going to happen with Cataclysma in the room."

"I'll make myow a better deal." Cataclysma says to Cobalt, "I'll cure myow of myow Tapeworms if myow kill all of them right neow."

"He's lying." Oscar says, "Myow can't cure Tapeworms."

"Yes but myow can weaken their immune systems so that certain medications can kill them." Cataclysma says, "It's technical but it can be done, and there's still time, but a deal is a deal…" he looks to Cobalt, "Kill them, submit to me, and I'll save myow from the splash."

Muffins goes to fire his gun but it clicks out. He throws it down and walks over grabbing the hot barrel of the gun in Cobalt's paw and pushing it up to Cobalt's face! "How about a face lift?" Muffins asks.

Cobalt swings to swat and Muffins jumps back quickly hissing! Muffins jumps forward and SWATs at Cobalt, ripping a line of Cobalt's skin open across the shoulder! It bleeds and it runs down his fur as he holds it with his paw, "Myow piece of shit!" he yells. Cobalt swings a knife at Muffins and it's dodged! Cobalt goes to stab Muffins but Muffins stops Cobalt's arm and Cobalt slams his paw up to Muffin's neck to the wall! Muffins SWATs Cobalt hard in the face and he steps back, they take stance and stare each other down with a groan and hiss. Muffins SWATs Cobalt again, SWAT! SWAT! SWAT! SWAT SWAT! Cobalt kicks up his hind legs and pounds Muffins face with his hind feet claws! Muffins Jumps at Cobalt and they tackle into a twisting chaotic hissing Meow-screeching fight with fur spots flying up in the air! Cobalt grabs a crow bar from the side of the garage laying next to him and swings it over pounds the bar into Muffins as he yelps loudly falling back onto the ground!

Muffins gets back up standing his ground in a moment of pause, they're both wounded. Cobalt completely exhausted and Muffins in pain, Cobalt looks over at Muffins and says, "I've always been smarter than myow. I'm an intellectual. I play chess, do crosswords and sudoku."

"Stop whining like myow had a traumatic experience." Muffins says.

"I did have a traumatic experience! I lost my wife to a car accident, myow butt hole!" Cobalt says sternly and dark.

Muffins insists, "Killing me won't un-kill myow pussy."

"And catching me won't bring back myow Space Police Station either. That entire entity is completey destroyed, and the handful of myow still chasing me down, are what's left of it. They might as well call myow, 'the Leftover Pussies'." Cobalt swings the crowbar at Muffins again and misses, again and misses, again and Muffin leaps forward at Cobalt on the swing into a tackle! Cobalt drops the crowbar and Muffins puts Cobalt into a sleeper-hold, holding him until he passes out.

Suddenly, a Tapeworm starts to splash out of Cobalt's butt hole and Muffins runs back quickly! Shallow, Oreo 7, and Oscar all open fire on both Cobalt's body and the Tapeworm, completely destroying whatever life may have been laying there approximately 10 seconds ago.

"Clear!" Shallow yells.

Maximus Cataclysma jumps into one of the cat hummers and slams the door, revving the engine, and screeching off out of the driveway! Oscar, Shallow, and Oreo 7 jump into the next hummer, while Muffins hooks the top end of Dr. Bonker's dolly to the trailer hitch of it, and they follow quickly behind with Dr. Bonkers meow screaming!

Just then, the entire Mansion explodes into a ball of flames for no, it just blows up, the statues, the windows blow out, the structural integrity completely disintegrates and it's really enjoyable to watch. Max puts the hummer into gear and peals out in the driveway, "Ehehehehe!" driving right through the front door of his own exploding mansion! The Extra Pussies drive swiftly behind, driven by Oscar!

Max drives the hummer out the back of the Mansion as it's on fire and Oscar drives in the hummer behind crashing through the house debris! One of the cats retrieves the duffle bag Muffins brought in and aims his own Bazooka at them as they chase Max in the hummer across the huge back porch! The cat fires the bazooka and the missile flies right in front of Oscar's wind shield, past the hummer, into the already exploding building, and exploding it even more; it could not explode more than it has now exploded.

With Max's hummer up ahead, Muffins gets parallel to Max's window, "Get me close to the car."

"Sure! Myow get to have all the fun, while I sit back and do nothing!" Oreo 7 says, "It's like I'm just here to watch!"

"Fine." He opens the door from inside the hummer, SWATs Oreo 7 across the face and pushes him out of the moving hummer! "Myow're fired." Muffins says. The door slams shut on its own from the turn as Oscar continues to follow Max! Oscar gets the hummer up next to Max's hummer and Muffins jumps onto the top of Max's hummer. Maximus Cataclysma says, "He always gets his cat, doesn't he?"

Max pulls a gun out and starts firing at the roof of the hummer! Muffins has to let go, so not to be hit by a bullet and hooks his paws on the edge at the back end of Max's hummer, swinging back in and holding on-busting in through the shattering back window! Max swings back and SWATs Muffins in the face good, and then SWATs him again; Max swerving and slamming into Oscar on the road! Muffins Bites Max's arm on the next SWAT and slams his impaling claws into Max's black fur coat, with his claws digging deeper than the coat and into Max's flesh as he meow-screams and the hummer speeds off road!

Max sees the Dark technology Collar on Muffins and grabs it with his nails, ripping it off Muffins quickly! Muffins SWATs Max across the Face again! SWAT! SWAT! SWAT SWAT SWAT!

Max jumps out of the hummer as its in full throttle into a forest of trees, tumbling and rolling and then jump up and running over to a dark under-shade from a pile of boulders, "Ehehehehe!" and disappears into the shadow! The Hummer slams into a tree and Muffins survives by slamming into the back of the front seat! He punches the door open and looks around for Max Cataclysma… as Oscar drove up… but Max… was gone.

Dr. Bonkers meow-screams from the dolly still hooked onto the trailer hitch.

16 ● THE DREAM

Oscar sat at the dining table in Shallows new apartment on the SS Pussy Willow. A lot of time had passed, possibly weeks, maybe a month. It was morning. Oscar was almost naked except for his fur and robe. He was sitting at the dining room table staring off into nothing, and Shallow came over to sit across the table from him with her mug of milk. She purrs and paws at Oscars paw. "Did myow sleep okay?" she asked him.

"Meh." Oscars says. "I had some like… dreams."

"Those are fairly common," Shallow says, "What did myow dream about?"

"Something interesting maybe…" Oscar says. "I had 2 dreams with my Dad in em'."

"…And…" she instigated.

"Well the first one I asked my Dad for some money and he called me a filthy loser and to get a job. But the second dream was like almost a memory cuz it was so realistic. I was out prowling on the land and the night fell and I still hadn't set up my camp shit yet. I was going through a pass in the mountains and it was myowkin' cold out there. There was snow everywhere- and then there's my *Dad*. He strolled past me without saying anything. He was looking pretty cold but he wouldn't look at me. By the looks of it, he was getting ready to camp out there in the dark with all that snow like a dumb idiot. I knew he was gonna be there for a while, I knew it like I already seen it happen. And then my alarm went off."

"What do myow think it means?" Shallow asks him.

Oscar looks out into a million mile stare and says, "It means, a Pussy's gotta survive. It means, that if I made him acknowledge me, he would've made me feel special. But then we'd set up camp, and he'd wait til I doze off. And then when I did, he'd sharpen his knife by the fire, and cut my heart out in my sleep. He'd eat my corpse, Shallow. Nothing can be wasted when myow starving. A pussy's gotta eat, Shallow. A pussy's gotta survive. We're all slaves, Shallow. Slaves to the tum tum."

Shallow says, "I'm going to order myow father a blanket."

...It might be continued. I don't know yet...

A special thanks to Alex Banchitta for inspiring me to dream up this ridiculous story.

The opinions and statements expressed herein are the responsibility of the author and are not necessarily endorsed by the publishers because they're humans.

Books by Daniel Jacobs Nÿkkýnn
America 51
Fatalgeist
My Current Opinion
Vein Cupid

For more information about any
of the above titles, visit:
nykkynn.com